Will You Still Love Me?

Jonathan stroked the side of Stephanie's face with his hand. "I need to tell you something. I hope what I say doesn't make you angry with me." Jonathan stopped and cleared his throat.

Warning bells went off inside Stephanie's head. What's he going to say, she wondered, instantly on guard. He's going to break it off. I knew it. I knew he was too good to be true. Stephanie steeled herself for what she thought Jonathan was going to say. But inside, her heart felt as if it were about to crumble.

"I realize we haven't known each other that long," Jonathan started again.

"No. Not long at all," Stephanie replied, her voice emotionless.

"But I'm falling in love with you, Stephanie," Jonathan said, staring straight into her eyes.

Stephanie drew in her breath sharply, then glanced up. She opened her mouth to say something, but nothing came out.

NANCY DREW ON CAMPUS™

1 New Lives, New Loves
2 On Her Own
3 Don't Look Back
4 Tell Me the Truth
5 Secret Rules
6 It's Your Move
7 False Friends
8 Getting Closer
9 Broken Promises
#10 Party Weekend
#11 In the Name of Love
#12 Just the Two of Us
#13 Campus Exposures
#14 Hard to Get
#15 Loving and Losing
#16 Going Home
#17 New Beginnings

Available from ARCHWAY Paperbacks

Nancy Drew on campus™ # 17

New Beginnings

Carolyn Keene

AN ARCHWAY PAPERBACK
Published by POCKET BOOKS
New York London Toronto Sydney Tokyo Singapore

AN ARCHWAY PAPERBACK *Original*

An Archway Paperback published by
POCKET BOOKS, a division of Simon & Schuster Inc.
1230 Avenue of the Americas, New York, NY 10020

Produced by Mega-Books, Inc.

ISBN: 0-671-56806-X

First Archway Paperback printing January 1997

10 9 8 7 6 5 4 3 2 1

Cover photos by Pat Hill Studio

Printed in the U.S.A.

IL 8+

Chapter 

You couldn't have come back at a better time, Bess," George Fayne said. "After tomorrow night's pep rally, Wilder U. becomes Party Central."

"Party Central," Nancy Drew repeated. "I like the sound of that." She leaned forward in the booth of the Copacetic Carrot, an off-campus health food restaurant where she and her two best friends were having an early lunch on Sunday.

Bess smiled weakly and held up her left arm, which was encased in a heavy white cast. "Hope this doesn't slow me down too much."

"Don't worry. You don't need your arm to cheer your head off at the rally," Nancy said. But when she looked at Bess's cast she shuddered inwardly. She hated remembering that awful day.

It had been less than a month ago that Bess had broken her arm. She and her boyfriend, Paul Cody, had been involved in a terrible motorcycle accident. Although Bess suffered only minor injuries, Paul had been killed. A devastated Bess had gone home to River Heights to recuperate.

Nancy thought about how worried she and George had been about Bess after the accident. The day Bess left campus, she'd told them she wasn't coming back to Wilder University. The memories would be too painful, she had said. Nancy and George had visited Bess in River Heights a week ago, hoping to convince her to come back to Wilder and to find out how she was feeling.

It had been a visit from Nancy's old boyfriend, Ned Nickerson, that got Bess to open up a little. Ned's heart-to-heart with Bess had helped change her mind about returning to Wilder, and Bess's parents had just driven her back to campus that morning.

Nancy looked up to see George patting Bess's cast. "Nancy's right, Bess. A little thing like a broken arm can't slow you down," George said. "Just sit back and let the parties come to you. Everyone's psyched that you're back."

"They are? That's nice," Bess said just as the waitress walked up to take their orders. Nancy noticed Bess didn't sound very sincere.

"So," Bess said after they had all ordered, "fill me in on what's been going on."

"Well," Nancy said brightly, propping her elbows on the table. "Jake and I have been keeping ourselves busy in the newsroom at the *Times.*" Nancy and her boyfriend, Jake Collins, were both reporters for the campus newspaper, the *Wilder Times.*

"And Will and I have been getting started on a new environmental science project," George said, shaking her short, dark curls. "But it's been hard to concentrate on it because it's more fun to focus on Will when I'm with him." She grinned.

Nancy and Bess both laughed. "That's not hard to believe, considering how gorgeous he is," Bess said. "With a boyfriend like Will, I wouldn't be able to think about school stuff either." Bess lowered her eyes to the tabletop, and Nancy watched a tear trickle down her left cheek.

Nancy and George were immediately ready to change the subject. Just then the waitress brought their salads.

"Hey, I talked to Eileen and Casey this morning," Nancy said, referring to two of her suitemates who belonged to the same sorority as Bess.

Bess's eyes lit up at the mention of her Kappa sorority sisters. "Did they know I was coming back?" Bess asked.

Nancy nodded. "That's all they could talk about. They can't wait to see you."

Color crept back into Bess's cheeks as they talked, and Nancy could see some of the old gleam take hold in her friend's eyes.

"They want you to stop by the Kappa house

this afternoon around four o'clock," Nancy said. "They've planned a little welcome-back celebration for you. No big deal. No pressure."

Bess bit her lip, obviously moved by the effort her sorority sisters were making. "I've missed them, too."

"So," George broke in, "we're going to yell our brains out at the pep rally tomorrow night. Then there's a football game the night after that. Aaaaand . . ." George paused dramatically and looked at Nancy.

"What?" Bess looked from one friend to the other.

"And there's tonight." Nancy smiled.

"More rallies?" Bess asked.

"No, a celebration." George tried to keep a straight face. "For you." She took a sip of her drink. "The Kappas passed on the news about your return to the guys at Zeta. They got hot to spring a big welcome-back party for you tonight. It's at the Underground." The Underground was a basement cafeteria by day that was transformed into one of the hottest places on campus at night, with a clublike atmosphere and live music.

"The Zetas want to do something for me? Really? That's so sweet."

Nancy nodded.

"And the party's tonight?" Bess asked. Nancy noticed that Bess seemed a little less than enthusiastic. "It sounds like fun. But that's a lot of parties in one day. And I probably should be hitting the books. I've missed so many classes."

This is so unlike you, Bess, Nancy thought. You always would have chosen a party over studying before Paul died. "You don't have to come if you're not ready," Nancy said out loud.

Maybe they'd planned too much, too soon. After all, Bess hadn't been anywhere near a party for a while. In fact, she'd spent the last couple of weeks recuperating, alone and depressed, in front of a TV set back in River Heights.

"Come on." George nudged Bess. "You don't really want to study tonight, do you?"

Bess gave her a nervous smile. "Okay. You're right. This will be good. It'll be fun."

"Now, if you could only figure out what to wear," George cracked.

"Exactly," Bess replied, a smile forming on her pale face. She tossed a balled-up napkin into George's lap. "That's half the fun!"

Nancy shook her head and laughed. George and Bess were cousins and close friends, but their personalities were miles apart. Outdoorsy George loved to party, but she'd just as soon show up in jeans with no makeup. Bess always lavished plenty of time on getting dressed for a party.

"So it's back to university life, Bess," Nancy kidded her. "All fun and games."

George groaned. "Yeah, right. I just remembered some annoying business I've got to take care of."

"What is it?" Nancy asked, checking her watch. She had to finish her latest feature article for the *Wilder Times* by this afternoon. *And* she wanted to see Jake. With any luck, he would be down at the newsroom, too.

George shrugged. "No big deal. I just had a phone message from the school bursar's office on Friday. Something about a problem with my bill for next semester's tuition."

"Don't tell me," Bess joked. "You took that big student loan and spent it all on clothes."

Nancy laughed. George was the last person on earth who would do anything crazy with money.

George tossed her head and laughed, too. "Nah. It's probably just a question about the loan servicing center I'm using to pay my bills. I'll call back tomorrow."

Nancy reached for her purse as the waitress slipped the tab onto the table. "Loan servicing center? What's that?"

George looked over at Nancy. "I got a letter from the student loan office recommending it. The deal is, I sign my loan check over to the servicing center, and they pay all my college expenses, like tuition and room and board."

"Did you send the servicing center your student loan check?" Bess asked.

"Yep," George answered, standing up with the others and stretching.

Nancy pushed the glass door open for George and Bess, and the three headed out onto the sunny sidewalk that led toward the campus. "Wonder what the problem could be," she said.

"It's nothing, I'm sure," George replied. "I'll call the bursar's office in the morning and get everything straightened out. I'd rather talk about Bess's Underground party—it's much more interesting."

"Okay," Bess said. "But let's get back to the dorm, George. I need to get unpacked."

"I have to get over to the newspaper office," Nancy said. "I'll see you guys later." She waved at her friends as she hurried off down the tree-lined street, happy to have Bess back on campus.

"That was a great sale you made earlier," Jonathan Baur said. "That woman with the gray hair."

Stephanie Keats nodded at her handsome boyfriend. "Yeah. She's a regular customer. And she likes *very* expensive cosmetics. Ninety-five dollars worth today."

Jonathan whistled and smiled. "Keep up the good work, and your manager might recommend you for a raise."

"Just watch your back," Stephanie deadpanned, flipping a strand of long, dark hair over her shoulder. "I might decide to go after your job."

"I'm not laughing," Jonathan said with admiration. "You could do it."

"Mmmm," Stephanie ran a shiny fingernail down Jonathan's neck. "I like a man who's not afraid of a challenge."

Stephanie felt a thrill run up her spine as Jonathan took her hand. The two walked slowly across downtown Weston's grassy square.

Tall, chestnut-haired Jonathan was a floor manager at Berrigan's department store, where Stephanie worked. In the past few weeks, their romance had started heating up. Last week, in fact, he'd given her a beautiful silver friendship ring, but Stephanie knew he thought of her as much more than a friend. And she felt the same way about him.

"Ten more minutes and our lunch hour will be over," Stephanie said, leaning her head against his shoulder as they walked. Looking over at Jonathan in his white dress shirt, tie, and brown slacks, Stephanie thought he seemed so much older and more sophisticated than the guys in the Wilder University dorm where she lived.

Jonathan turned and caught her staring at him. His eyes crinkled up with a sudden smile. "What are you thinking?"

Stephanie hesitated. She wasn't sure she wanted Jonathan to know how strongly she felt about him. He was the first guy she had ever fallen in love with, but she was afraid to admit it. Maybe other women in her dorm could take chances with relationships, but she was different.

"Stephanie?" She heard Jonathan's voice floating into her thoughts. He'd stopped walking. A sturdy arm slipped across her back. When she turned to him, she saw that his eyes had softened and that his mouth was tight with emotion. He seemed to be about to say something important. A slight breeze blew a few strands of hair across

Stephanie's face, and Jonathan leaned in to brush them away.

"Stephanie, I—I just wanted to say I've never met anyone quite like you," Jonathan began, taking her face and cradling it in one hand.

A delicious wisecrack was on the tip of Stephanie's tongue, but she held back when she saw the expression in Jonathan's eyes.

Jonathan took his other hand and stroked the side of her face. "I need to tell you something. I hope what I say doesn't make you angry with me." Jonathan stopped and cleared his throat.

Warning bells went off inside Stephanie's head. What's he going to say, she wondered, instantly on guard. He's going to break it off. I knew it. I knew Jonathan was too good to be true. Stephanie steeled herself for what she thought he was going to say. But inside, her heart felt as if it were about to crumble.

"I realize we haven't known each other that long," Jonathan started again.

"No. Not long at all," Stephanie replied, her voice emotionless.

"But I'm falling in love with you, Stephanie," Jonathan said, staring straight into her eyes.

Stephanie drew in her breath sharply, then glanced up. She opened her mouth to say something, but nothing came out. Jonathan falling in love with her? This was definitely not what she'd expected. She hadn't realized until that moment how much she'd wanted to hear him say that.

"I, uh, I . . ." Stephanie stammered, turning to face him.

Gently Jonathan stopped her from speaking by placing his hand over her mouth. "Don't say anything yet. Just think about it."

Stephanie felt his arms wrap around her. And she no longer could think of anything to say. Jonathan's long, passionate kiss had completely silenced her.

George tightened the laces on her running shoes as she sat on a grassy patch next to the Mall, a wide walkway lined with university buildings at the center of campus.

She lowered herself into a deep hamstring stretch. Since meeting with Nancy and Bess at the Copacetic Carrot, she'd felt restless and a little overwhelmed. In addition to her loan matters to straighten out, she had to study and attend parties for the next two nights in a row. She wondered how she was going to get everything done.

Still, George reflected, as she reached high overhead to stretch her arms, at least Bess seemed to be on the road to recovery. Right now that was more important to her than anything. Besides, she had a five-mile run ahead of her, and running always took her mind off her problems.

She saw Pam Miller and Eileen O'Connor moving toward her across the campus lawn. "Hi," George's roommate, Pam, said, sitting next to George on the grass. She was wearing a red tank top and blue silk running shorts. Her long, dark legs gleamed in the sun. Like George, she was into all kinds of sports and was also serious about academics. She slipped a tube of lip balm out of her fanny pack. "Eileen's catching up."

A second later a squarely built girl with blond hair and hazel eyes bounded up. "Don't gloat because you've got twice the speed I have," she called out good-naturedly, flopping down onto the grass.

Pam smiled. "I'm not gloating."

Eileen laughed and pointed a finger at Pam. "You're gloating because you're in perfect shape. But I've got endurance, and I will stick with you for all five miles."

"Stretch," George ordered.

"How's Bess?" Pam wanted to know.

"She's going to be fine," George replied. "In fact, she's joining us tonight at the Underground for her welcome-back party—so make sure you're both there. We'll tear up the place."

Eileen's eyes lit up. Her face was flushed under a spray of freckles. "Oh, good. I'm glad she went for the idea."

"So much to do and so little time," Pam said with a sigh, her eyes following a slender, well-built guy approaching them on the Mall walkway. "Mmmm. I know that guy. But I can't remember from where."

George studied him, too. He had wavy, light brown hair and a delicate, unassuming face. "Yeah. I recognize him, but my brain's too fried right now to place him."

"Jamal works with him," Pam said, suddenly remembering. She was referring to her boyfriend, Jamal Lewis. She zipped her fanny pack shut and caught his eye with a wave.

"Hi," the guy said with a friendly nod as he strode past the girls.

"Hi," Pam called back. "Jamal introduced us a few weeks back. You work with him at the student loan office, don't you?"

"Yeah." The guy stopped and took a moment to think. Then his face brightened and he approached, pointing playfully. "I remember you. You're Pam, Jamal's girlfriend. I'm Greg Pawling."

"Right, Greg." Pam nodded as the guy knelt down next to her. "This is George Fayne and Eileen O'Connor."

"Hi." George smiled before grabbing her knee and dropping her head to it for another deep stretch.

"Would you please tell Jamal to stop working such long hours?" Pam teased. "I never get to see him anymore."

Greg laughed. "Yeah, it's tough all around, but I'm not complaining. I'm in grad school now, and I've got bills to pay."

George sighed. Why was everyone suddenly talking about bills?

"Hey." Greg's face lit up as his eyes flicked from George to Pam to Eileen. "Have you heard about Club Z? It's a new dance club opening up next week in downtown Weston. I just came from there."

"Are you kidding? I've heard about nothing else from Jason Lehman the last few weeks," Eileen said, her eyes shining. She sat up and crossed her legs.

"You know Jason?"

Eileen nodded. "I've been dating his brother Emmet. He took me to see the club. It's a great space for live music, and it's going to have a huge dance floor."

"That sounds great!" George was psyched. "Will and I love to dance."

Greg nodded and stood up. "I've been helping out with the renovations and setup. There are some great bands booked for the first month. Come check it out."

"Okay. See you there, Greg," Pam said as Greg hurried across the lawn toward the Math and Sciences Building. Then she turned to George and Eileen and jogged around them in her running shoes. "Come on, you guys. Let's get this run over with. It'll give us more energy to party."

"It might give you two more, but I don't know if it'll help me," Eileen replied, following Pam as she took off.

Laughing, George sprang up and shook her arms out before heading across the leafy campus.

Chapter 2

Bess hugged her purse to her chest as she hurried down a shady off-campus street toward the Kappa house. The day had been nerve-racking, with everyone treating her like an invalid. During the drive back to Wilder with her parents, Bess's mother kept telling her to be careful with her broken arm, and her father just sat stonily silent, his jaw clenched with worry.

Then, as soon as she arrived on campus, Nancy and George had dragged her to the Copacetic Carrot. Their worried expressions and too-obvious attempts to cheer her up had only made her feel uncomfortable. Bess sighed. She knew everyone cared about her and wanted to help, but she hated all their worrying.

She made a quick trip to the dorm, emptied her mailbox, and left a note for her roommate,

Leslie King. Now she was off to see her sorority sisters at Kappa. Bess prayed they weren't going to tiptoe around her.

She headed up the front walk of the Kappa house past the square hedges, and onto the front steps of the old Victorian. Music floated out of the second-story windows.

"Bess!" She heard a shouted greeting as the front door swung open. Bess smiled broadly as her sorority sisters, Holly Thornton and Casey Fontaine, emerged onto the large old porch. Bess could see the concern on their faces as they drew near.

"How are you?" Holly asked softly, stepping forward and giving Bess a long, careful hug. Her brown eyes searched Bess's. "Welcome back."

Bess bit her lip, feeling uncomfortable. "I'm fine. Really."

Casey slipped an arm around her waist and guided her up the stairs to the door. With her short, red hair and funky clothes, Casey was usually a bundle of sparks and energy. Today, however, she was subdued. "Don't worry. You can just be yourself. Okay?" she said with a tender smile. "Are you hungry? Does your arm hurt?"

Bess stared at Casey and Holly. "No. I'm fine." Then she glanced up and saw the strained faces of the other Kappas gathered at the front door. Their faces reminded Bess of those of her parents and Nancy and George.

"Hi, you guys," she said brightly, walking through the door and into the front room. Everyone trailed behind her. Bess tried to break the ice with a smile. "It's so good to see this place again. It looks great, as always." She glanced around at the comfortable assortment of easy chairs, bookshelves, and tables. Freshly cut flowers were everywhere, and a big buffet and tea service had been laid out in the dining room.

"Hi, Bess. Welcome back." Bess was surprised to see Soozie Beckerman, the secretary of the Kappas. She was walking into the dining room with a silver tray of cookies in her hands. Normally, Soozie wouldn't be caught dead serving cookies, or, for that matter, welcoming Bess to anything.

"I hope you're okay," Soozie said, giving Bess an encouraging smile. "Does your arm hurt?" Bess shook her head, then shifted uncomfortably as everyone gathered around the table. They were all acting so weird. She wished someone would start talking about the latest party, or some cute guy, or any subject that wasn't about her.

Holly cleared her throat to speak. "On behalf of the Kappas, Bess, we'd just like to say, 'Welcome back.' We know you've been through a lot, and we want you to let us know if we can help."

"We're here for you, Bess," another Kappa said, staring worriedly at Bess's cast.

Bess smiled politely. "Thank you."

"If you need help with any of your classwork, I'm there for you," Casey piped up.

"Yeah," another voice joined in. "Any time you want to borrow anything, just drop by, Bess."

"Um, thanks," Bess replied, fingering her purse and wondering what she was supposed to do next. She'd been looking forward to seeing her Kappa sisters again, but she hadn't expected this. It almost felt to her as if they wanted her to cry or collapse on the floor.

"Hi, everyone." She heard Eileen's confident voice at the front door. Bess relaxed. Maybe Eileen could rescue her. "Hey—is everyone ready for Bess? She's supposed to . . ." Eileen's voice trailed off.

Bess turned around and smiled, but the expression on Eileen's face, flushed from running, suddenly became serious. "Oh, Bess. You're *here. Everyone's* here. Well, that's great. Just great." Bess thought Eileen looked as if she was afraid to get near her.

Bess cringed.

"Help yourself, you guys," Casey was saying, pouring tea as everyone began talking quietly around the big dining room table. "Just make sure Bess gets a cup of tea and some cookies. And don't bump her cast!"

Bess sat down in a chair, trying to look inconspicuous. Holly knelt down next to her. "We're planning a *real* welcome-back party for you later in the week. Sorry this isn't much, but we didn't have time."

"No . . ." Bess tried to protest, nearly choking on the bite of cookie she'd just taken.

"What?" Holly seemed worried.

"I—I mean . . ." Bess stammered. "This is great, Holly." Bess raised her voice a little when she realized that the other Kappas were staring at her. "This is really wonderful. Thanks so much. But you don't need to throw another party for me. There's one at the Underground tonight, isn't there?"

"Yes!" everyone chorused instantly.

"But, Bess," Eileen insisted, "we wanted to give you a *special* welcome back."

Bess wanted to laugh, but everyone seemed so concerned, she was almost embarrassed to. Instead, she straightened her back and put on the most confident smile she could manage. "This *is* special. But I really have to start spending some serious time at the library."

She watched her sorority sisters exchange concerned glances. "Hey, I can't party *all* the time, can I?"

There was a long silence during which everyone avoided her eyes. Suddenly Eileen accidentally knocked over her full teacup onto a stack of magazines.

"Jeez, good one," Eileen said as she jumped up to clean up the wet mess. A couple of girls scrambled to pull magazines out of the way, while others went to the kitchen to get towels. Everyone seemed to be relieved by the interruption.

During all the commotion, Bess slipped out of the room into the front hallway. She let out a deep breath and leaned back against the wall.

She had hoped the Kappas would have been able to treat her normally.

Closing her eyes in frustration, Bess found the image of Paul's handsome face floating in front of her. She opened them again, now on the verge of tears. Settling back into her old life wasn't going to be easy.

Ray Johansson cupped two hands around his tall double espresso and stared at the groups of students trickling in through the glass doors of Java Joe's, a Wilder campus hangout.

He clenched his jaw and forced himself to stare back down at the book he was trying to finish. It was late, and by this time, the place was starting to fill with an assortment of refugees from the dorms and library study carrels. For the first time since the semester began, Ray found himself alone, without his band, and without Ginny.

Ray tried to focus on the book, but all he could think about was his former band, the Beat Poets, out in sunny Los Angeles, probably jamming right now with a bunch of big-name artists after a tough day of recording at Pacific Records.

He gulped his espresso and leaned way back in his chair. Things had been great until a week ago, when the Pacific Records executives told him they wanted his friend Spider Kelly to take over as lead singer for the band. When Ray refused to go along with the plan, he was fired. The Beat Poets had been his creation, and now he was kicked out and without a band.

On top of everything else, Ray and his girlfriend, Ginny Yuen, had decided not to see each other for a while, and he was regretting this decision. They were still friendly, but everytime he saw her with Frank Chung, he felt as if someone had hit him in the stomach. This afternoon he'd had the bad luck of spotting them walking into the library together.

"Mr. Straight Arrow, Frank Chung," Ray muttered under his breath. "Ginny's parents must be dancing in the streets."

"Hey, Ray." He heard a breathy voice behind him. "What's going on?"

Ray turned and glanced at the slender, blond girl standing next to his table. She wore a clingy, black leotard top and tight jeans.

"Mind if I sit down?" she asked. "Do you remember me? I'm Montana Smith."

Ray tried to focus. "Oh, yeah," he answered, motioning to the chair across from his. "I met you over at Thayer Hall. You're Kara Verbeck's friend."

"Sorority sister, too," Montana said, settling into her chair with a dry smile. Her eyes seemed to wait for his reaction while she unhooked her purse and set it down next to her. "And I know Ginny, too."

Ray cleared his throat. "Right."

Montana twisted a lock of her curly hair around one finger. Ray was starting to wonder why she sat down with him. He was in no mood to make small talk.

"Want some coffee?" Ray finally asked.

"No, thanks," Montana said lightly, still focusing on him. She paused, then leaned forward on her elbows. "Sorry about your band."

Ray took a final swig of his coffee and set it down. He raked his short, black hair back with his fingers. "Yeah. My own fault."

Montana continued to stare, and Ray could see that her eyes were a stunning, icy blue. "I'd say bad luck."

"Whatever."

"Fired from your own band," Montana went on. "That's really lousy."

Ray glanced over at the next table, his stomach beginning to knot up.

"I heard the Beat Poets a lot when you were together," Montana explained. "I loved your sound. And you wrote all of your own music, didn't you?"

"Yep," Ray said shortly, and turned away. "Lot of good that did me."

"Look," Montana finally said. "I wanted you to know about a band I heard last week." Her eyes sparkled. "Um. Maybe you know that I spend a lot of time down at the campus radio station. I've got a new call-in show with Kara and Nikki Bennett?"

Ray nodded. "Yeah. I heard about it. Pretty funny, I guess."

Montana grinned. "I love it." Her expression got serious again. "Anyway. I heard a really great local band last week when they came into the station for an interview—just before our show started. I listened to their tape, and they're really, really good. A strong, driving beat, but with a message. You know?"

Ray shrugged.

"So"—Montana leaned over the table conspiratorially—"I talked to one of the band members, Cory McDermott. The band is breaking up."

Ray looked at her.

Montana wriggled a little in her seat. "It got me thinking, Ray. If you ever wanted to start another band, you might want to look him up. Believe me, he's really hot."

Ray whistled and shook his head. He leaned back in his chair and stuffed his hands into the pockets of his jeans. "It's pretty hard to think of playing with anyone but the Beat Poets."

Montana's pretty mouth dropped open a little, and she seemed to be surprised. A moment later she put her hand lightly over his. "You're not going to drop your music forever, are you, Ray?"

Ray glanced down at her hand. "Well, no . . ."

"Good," Montana said with a confident smile. She stood up to leave. "When you want to meet Cory, you let me know. Okay?"

"Okay," Ray said, suddenly realizing that Montana had lifted his spirits. "Okay, I will. And thanks."

Nancy squeezed through the crowd at the Underground. Onstage, three girls in black, playing acoustic guitars, belted out a fast dance tune.

"Hi, Nancy!" a guy from one of her classes called out over the music.

Nancy grinned and pushed through the mass of bodies, straining for a glimpse of Bess and George. The lights were dimmed, and rows of tiny, white lights edged the low ceiling. Each table glowed from the light of a single candle in a glass bowl.

Nancy felt herself give in to the music and the crowd as she searched for her friends. She waved at a table jammed with friends from Thayer Hall. Then she took a deep breath. It had been a wild afternoon.

After her lunch with Bess and George, she'd hurried down to the newsroom and finished a story. Then, after a rushed dinner, she'd driven downtown to pay a quick farewell visit to twelve-year-old Anna Pederson and her father. Nancy had been Anna's big sister through a volunteer program called Helping Hands. Anna and her dad were moving to another town, where he'd found a new job.

"*Nancy.*" She heard George's voice calling her above the noise. "Over here."

Spotting George at a table near the stage, Nancy waved. She gave George a cheerful, I-give-up sign, since a blockade of bodies and chairs wasn't going to allow her to get near George any-time soon.

Nancy then noticed her boyfriend, Jake Collins, standing and waving at her from a table on the other side of the room. She took in his rumpled brown hair, gray T-shirt, jeans, and cowboy boots, and her heart speeded up as it always did when she saw him. But then she tensed, thinking of the problems they'd had lately. As she watched, he grinned and pointed to the empty chair next to him. She put on a smile and waved.

As she started across the room, she heard a deep voice behind her. She felt a strong hand on her arm and turned.

"Terry, hi." Nancy's smile grew bigger. Terry Schneider was a tall, sandy-haired guy she knew through the Focus Film Society, a campus group that showed screenings of classic movies. The music stopped, and the room was suddenly filled with talking and laughter.

"How've you been?" Terry asked. He brushed a loose strand of hair off his forehead. He nodded toward a table of Kappas. "I'm a Kappa date tonight, you see."

Nancy laughed. "Hey, that's great." She threw a nervous glance over at Jake, who was watching from across the room.

"So," Terry said with a sly look. "Where's Jake?"

"There." Nancy pointed across the room and waved again at Jake. Turning back to Terry, she noticed again his resemblance to her old boyfriend, Ned Nickerson. Terry had the same height, athletic build, and square jaw. Even the polo shirt Terry wore looked as if it had come straight from Ned's closet. A few weeks earlier she and Terry had spent time together during a special film event sponsored by the Focus Film Society. Jake had been a little jealous.

Nancy knew Jake was probably watching from across the room, but she tried to shrug it off. She liked Terry as a friend. What could be wrong with that?

"Did you see *Five Riders* down at the Weston?" Terry quizzed her.

Nancy nodded. "Loved it."

"You're kidding."

Nancy shook her head. "No. I loved the story. It kept me guessing every minute. I still haven't figured it out."

"Cheap violence for the sake of violence," Terry shouted as the music started again."

"Sorry, Ne—Terry," Nancy insisted, folding her arms over her chest, embarrassed that she'd almost called him Ned. "You're much too afraid of the offbeat in film."

"I've led a sheltered life," Terry yelled back with a laugh. It was too loud to talk, so they just smiled for a moment, until Terry's grin faded and his gaze shifted over her shoulder.

"Nan." She heard Jake's voice and turned around. Jake was right behind her, smiling under a tangle of brown hair. He lifted his hand to greet Terry. They really don't have much in common, Nancy thought. Jake was quick-thinking, intense, and passionately driven about his work for the *Wilder Times*. He wanted a career as a hard-nosed reporter on a big-city paper someday.

Terry tended to be on the creative, fun-loving side and was working toward a life in film.

"I was saving a place for you, Nan," Jake said into her ear, nuzzling it a little. At Jake's touch, a surge of electricity ran through Nancy. Abruptly she felt awkward with Terry standing right there.

" 'Bye, Terry," she said, taking a step toward Jake. "Have fun tonight."

She walked ahead of Jake and felt his hand on her back, making her spine tingle as they wove back through the crowd. In the distance she spotted Bess holding court with her broken arm. She was surrounded by a group of guys from the Zeta house.

Finally they found their seats, and Jake took Nancy's hand. The toe of his cowboy boot was tapping in time to the music, but Nancy sensed that the tension between them wasn't over. It had started the weekend before, when they'd gone to her home in River Heights to visit with her dad.

To Nancy's surprise, her father's new girlfriend, Avery, had been with them every moment of the weekend. Although she liked Avery, Nancy had suddenly felt like a guest in her own home, and she hadn't liked that.

To make things worse, Jake seemed totally unable to understand Nancy's feelings about the situation. It made her realize how new her relationship with Jake was. After all, when she bumped into Ned that weekend, *he'd* totally understood how she felt.

"Hel-*lo*," Jake was saying into her ear. He kissed the side of her neck.

Nancy shivered. Sharp-tongued, clever Jake. He didn't always understand her, but she couldn't deny the sparks that flew between them whenever they were together. They probably just needed more time, Nancy told herself. Everything will work out—right?

Stephanie crossed her legs and sat back in her chair, taking in the crazed Underground scene spread out before her. It had been hours since Jonathan had made his stunning confession of love. Her heart was full, but she still didn't know whether to bounce off the walls with glee or run away in terror. She knew she loved Jonathan, but tonight she needed to clear her head. So she'd come to the Underground alone.

"Stephanie?" Kara Verbeck was calling out over the music. "Stephanie? Are you there?"

Stephanie slid her eyes toward Kara, who was sitting with some girls from Stephanie's suite in Thayer Hall. "I'm here," Stephanie answered in an annoyed tone of voice.

Kara smiled. "It's just that we've been trying to get your attention, and you're obviously thinking about something else."

"Some*one* else, I think," the resident adviser for Thayer Hall, Dawn Steiger, said, studying Stephanie.

"You guys are so insightful," Stephanie said. "It really blows me away." Suddenly restless,

Stephanie flipped back her hair and tried to ignore her suitemates. She gripped the sides of her chair and drummed her fingernails on its underside.

She still couldn't believe Jonathan had actually confessed that he was in love with her. Tall, sophisticated Jonathan Baur. It was too much to begin to contemplate. It was wonderful, yes. But there was something else, too. Something scary and strange that made her stop right in the middle of the hallway that afternoon when she was about to phone Jonathan and invite him to the Underground party for Bess.

"She's not talking," Kara teased.

"Nope," Dawn agreed.

Stephanie unzipped the tiny belt pack she wore around her skintight, Lycra mini-dress. Then she took out a cigarette and lit it up. "Back off," she said, glancing at them briefly.

"Come on, Steph," Kara said innocently. "Where is he?"

Stephanie glared at the two, stood up, and leaned against the table, her eyes roaming the room. She'd never tell her friends that she was scared stiff, that she loved Jonathan and wanted to figure out how to have a relationship with him and be happy. But she had no idea what she was supposed to do next. She felt as if she was losing control.

"That guy over there is staring at you, Stephanie." Kara was nudging her. "Check him out."

Stephanie felt herself go on autopilot. Swiveling around, she crossed one leg over the other, revealing most of her thigh. Then she caught the guy's eye and found herself liking what she saw. Curly, dark hair, full lips, and a look of longing that instantly drew her.

She watched, and then without thinking or feeling, she made her move and strolled across the room. "Hi," the guy said. He was leaning against the bar at the back of the room, staring openly at her tight dress.

Stephanie felt the familiar thrill. "Hello," she said. "I'm Stephanie." She forced herself to push thoughts of Jonathan out of her mind.

The guy gave her a wide smile and slipped an arm around her waist. "I'm Mike."

Stephanie threw a cool stare at the guys lined up at the bar next to Mike. They were gawking at her and nudging one another. "Don't mean to intrude, Mike," Stephanie said dryly.

"Let's talk over there," Mike called out above the roar of the music. He pulled her away out of the jostling crowd into a dark, quiet corner on the other side of a phone booth. Suddenly face-to-face, Stephanie felt the old confidence take over.

"That looks good," Stephanie said, throwing her cigarette down and crushing it. She looked at his drink.

"I'll share," Mike said with a sultry look, handing her his plastic cup.

Stephanie took the cup and drew its straw to her lips. Then she took a long drink, all the time staring into his eyes.

"Mmmmm," Stephanie murmured. "I was thirsty."

"I am, too, Stephanie," Mike murmured back. He took the cup from her and set it down on a chair next to them. Then he slid both hands around her waist and up her back until her chest was pressed into his. His kiss was long and deep, and Stephanie felt herself give in to it. This was more like it. No thoughts of love. Now she was in control again. Wasn't she?

Chapter 3

Will Blackfeather wrapped his muscular arms around George's waist and nuzzled the back of her neck. "Walk with me to class."

George shivered and checked her watch. "I don't have time. I've only got twenty minutes until my ten o'clock class, and I have to make a phone call before I leave."

"George," Will said softly, turning her around and kissing her. His smooth skin was coppery against his white T-shirt, and his dark eyes glowed above his high cheekbones. "You have time. I'll wait."

"Mmmm," George relaxed against him for a moment before pulling away. "I like the way you put that."

Sinking down into a chair in the corner of Will's small apartment, George pulled a slip of paper with a phone number on it from her purse. "I've got some business with the student bursar's office to take care of," she said, dialing the phone.

George stared at Will as he gathered up his books. Just looking at him made her want to forget everything else. Sometimes she wished weekends could last forever.

"Yes?" A man answered the phone.

George took a breath. "My name is George Fayne. I had a call from your office concerning my bill for next semester."

There was a pause on the other end of the line. "Just a moment while I get your file," the man said.

"Oh, yes," he said, coming back on the line. "George Fayne."

"Right," George replied.

"We haven't received the money for your tuition and room and board fees for the next semester. It was due last week," the man said.

"Yes, I've already sent my loan check over to the University Loan Servicing Center," George explained.

"The what?"

"The University Loan Servicing Center," she replied. "Your office sent me a letter recommending that I sign my loan check over to the center so they could distribute my funds—"

"Young lady," the man interrupted, "I have never heard of the University Loan Servicing Center, and we'd certainly never recommend that students sign their loan checks over to anyone but Wilder University."

George's heart skipped a beat. "But I—"

"Ms. Fayne," the man interrupted again, "this office sent your bill with instructions—as always—to send your money to this office. We have not changed any payment policies here at Wilder, *and* we have not received your funds."

"But I—"

"If you can't straighten this matter out, I'm afraid you won't be able to register for next semester's classes."

"I'm glad you're back," Brian Daglian said, letting out a sigh and giving Bess a hug as they walked down the Mall after their psych class. "When do you get that thing off?" he asked, examining her heavy cast.

"In a couple of weeks," Bess said. "I can't wait."

Brian nodded sympathetically. "You know, I really missed you. I had to suffer through auditions and classes all by myself."

Bess rolled her eyes. "You're never by yourself, Brian."

Brian laughed. "True. I guess I prefer friends to solitude. Maybe that's why I like the theater."

Bess laughed. Brian always managed to cheer her up. She took in his golden hair, sea green eyes, and big, boyish smile. Then she nudged him with her hip. She and Brian had been good friends ever since her first week at Wilder University.

Brian checked his watch. "We'll make it on time if we walk fast."

Bess slowed, shifting her book pack on her good shoulder.

"Come on," Brian urged. "Lunch with Casey and Chris. I'll carry the pack. It'll be fun."

"I've got to study, Brian," Bess protested. She'd been at home for a couple of weeks, staring at soap operas and seeing no one. Then on her first day back, she'd been partied to death with the tea at the Kappa house, and the welcome-back celebration by the Zetas at the Underground. She was tired of socializing, especially with everyone still acting as if she were made of glass.

Brian grabbed her elbow and pulled her ahead. "Chris is dying to see you."

"Chill out, Brian," Bess snapped. She winced inwardly when she saw Brian look pained. She hadn't meant to sound so harsh. It was just that she'd seen Casey twice since yesterday. And she couldn't face the thought of Brian's close friend, Chris Vogel, looking at her with an "Oh, poor Bess" expression, which she was sure he'd do.

"Sorry, Bess," Brian said quietly. "I was just trying to help."

Bess sighed. "I'm really sorry, Brian. I just need time, okay? And today I need to study. I know that doesn't sound much like the old, crazy me. But I've missed weeks of school."

Brian gave her an affectionate squeeze, then planted a quick kiss on her cheek. "Get going, I can take it."

Bess waved, and hurried toward Jamison Hall, the dorm where she lived. She kept her head down, ignoring the bands of Frisbee players criss-crossing the lawn and walkways to the dorms. Part of her didn't want to talk to another soul for a month. Another part of her wanted to connect again with someone—maybe even the way she'd connected with Paul.

She closed her eyes, praying she could make her way to her dorm room without bumping into another one of Paul's sympathetic frat brothers. Or another Kappa sister with advice on grieving, mourning, and validating one's feelings.

All she wanted to do right now was forget and have everyone else forget, too. But everywhere she turned there was a reminder of Paul. The Kappa and Zeta houses, where they'd been to so many parties. The Underground, where they'd danced and shared a hundred kisses. Even walking back to her room reminded her of the way she used to hope he'd left a phone message or a note.

Bess dug for her key as she raced up the front steps. Now, on top of everything, everyone wanted to cheer her up. Couldn't they just let her feel sad for a while?

"At last." Bess breathed a sigh of relief, closing her dorm room door. She walked over to the window that looked out over the campus. At least she didn't have to pretend everything was okay here, she thought, yanking the curtains closed. Turning away, she fell wearily onto her narrow bed and felt tears gather in her eyes. There was a sound at the door, and Bess tried to blink the tears away.

"Hi," she heard her roommate, Leslie King, call out as she came into the room.

Bess slowly opened her eyes and looked at Leslie's concerned face. Her straight, brown hair was pulled back and up into a tight ponytail, and when Leslie turned on the lamp next to the bed, Bess could see every line in her worried brow.

"I came straight back from my calculus class to see if you were okay."

Bess tried to breathe normally through her tears. "I'm okay. Really."

Leslie bit her bottom lip and said nothing.

Bess sighed. "Please, Leslie. I'm fine. I just came back to the room to do some studying."

Leslie acted unconvinced. Sitting on the edge of Bess's bed, she put her elbows on her knees and played with the buttons on her navy polo shirt. "Studying," she echoed softly.

Exasperated, Bess sat up. Yes, studying, Bess thought. Was it really that incredible?

"Classes were a real bear this morning." She tried to make light conversation. "It's hard getting back."

Leslie looked her straight in the eye. "Bess," she said, "I can see you've been crying."

Bess's lower lip quivered. "I'm all right. Look, I'll get through this."

Leslie sat down next to her and gave her a tissue. "Alone?"

"Alone?" Bess faced her. "I haven't been alone since I arrived back on campus."

"People want to help."

"Well, they can't," Bess said fiercely. "No one can help. No one can bring Paul back. No one can magically send me back in time, so Paul and I could decide to stay home that day instead of borrowing Will's motorcycle to go for a drive. And no one can stop Zach Bainbridge from going through that intersection and smashing into the bike."

"I know that, Bess," Leslie said quietly. "I'm just saying that you're not alone."

"But I *want* to be alone," Bess replied, springing up and grabbing a tissue to blow her nose. "It just makes things worse when people treat me with kid gloves. It reminds me of everything."

"Oh, Bess," Leslie said. "I'm sorry."

Something clutched at Bess's throat. She sat down at her desk chair. "I miss him, Leslie. I miss Paul," she said as the tears started again.

Leslie sat very still while Bess finished crying. "Do you remember what you told me when I was going through that horrible time a while ago?"

"I told you to get some counseling," Bess replied.

Leslie nodded. "Right. And you even walked me down to the student health center."

"Yes," Bess replied. "My parents want me to see a counselor, too."

Leslie looked Bess in the eye. "The counselor *really* helped me figure things out and understand a lot of stuff about myself."

Leslie took a pencil from her desk drawer and wrote something down on a card. "Here's my counselor's name and number," she said. Then she stuffed her hands in the pockets of her chinos and flopped back on her own bed.

"Thanks," Bess said lightly, taking the card. "I'll see if I can fit it into my study schedule. I've got a lot of catching up to do."

Leslie slipped a heavy textbook out of her bookbag and settled it on her lap. "We had some new heavy-duty lab work last week in biology. You'll probably have to make it up."

Bess cringed.

"You can do it," Leslie urged.

"I've got too much to do," Bess said, starting to panic. Leslie was in the same biology class, so Bess knew she'd get plenty of help. But there were other classes, too. How would she ever catch up?

"Look what I have for you," Leslie said, holding up some colorful papers. "These are study sheets I put together. They're color-coded."

Bess stared at the neatly typed pages with a sinking heart. What was she getting herself into? She had never been into studying like this.

Leslie was explaining, "Pink for high-priority

concepts, blue for examples, and green for terminology."

Bess read them over, suddenly cheered. "It makes it look so—manageable," Bess murmured, thinking it wasn't as weird as she first thought.

Leslie peeled open a pack of gum. "Nothin' to it."

Bess settled in with the study sheets and glanced at the clock. Studying would be better than thinking about Paul and feeling the pitying looks on her back.

It was hard for even Bess to believe, but she was anxious to study.

Stephanie stuck her blow dryer, makeup kit, and brush in her bag, padded out of the dorm bathroom, and headed down the hall. It was Monday morning, and her eyelids were sagging. She'd stayed out until one o'clock in the morning, making out with Mike in a dim corner of the Underground. Somehow her roommate, Casey Fontaine, had managed to drag her away from him, and when they'd returned to the dorm, there had been two messages on her machine from Jonathan.

She tried to pretend that everything was normal. But deep down she knew that something was terribly wrong.

"He told me he loved me," Stephanie whispered to herself, opening the door to her room. Lots of guys had told her they'd loved her. But Stephanie knew Jonathan was the first guy who really meant it. What was wrong with her? Why did she feel that she had to run away from Jonathan and take up with the first cute guy to smile at her from across a crowded room?

Stephanie dumped her stuff on her bed.

"Hi," Casey greeted her. Casey was sitting cross-legged on her own bed, dabbing a toenail with a vivid shade of purple while trying to read a paperback.

"Hi," Stephanie muttered, flinging open her closet door.

Casey blew on her toes and closed the bottle of polish. Then she stood up and stretched. Over gray sweats she was wearing an oversize T-shirt that read The President's Daughter in pink script above a silk screen of her own face. Before enrolling at Wilder, Casey had been a teen TV star, playing the lead in a hit television series.

The phone rang and Stephanie jumped.

"Hello?" Casey answered.

Stephanie prayed it wasn't Jonathan.

"Oh, hi, Jonathan," Casey said loudly, twisting around to give Stephanie a look.

Stephanie waved her arms wildly and shook her head.

"Yes," Casey said firmly, "she's right here."

Stephanie could feel her heart beating in her throat. But she sucked in a deep breath and took the phone. She was going to have to be very cool. There was no way Jonathan could ever find out what had happened the night before with Mike.

"Hi, Jonathan." Stephanie tried to sound normal.

"Hi, beautiful," Jonathan said gently. "I just got to work and wanted to say hi."

Stephanie felt a tug. Just hearing his voice flooded her with feelings for him. She could never, *ever* jeopardize their relationship again. And this would be the last time she'd ever have to lie to him. "Sorry I missed your call," Stephanie said softly. "I was in the library until all hours last night."

Casey was rolling her eyes.

"You must be beat," Jonathan sympathized.

"Yeah," Stephanie replied, choked with guilt. "I ran into Nancy after dinner, and she reminded me of a western civ paper due this afternoon. I'd almost blown the whole thing off. She offered to help, as long as we could work in the library."

"I love you, Steph."

"Ditto, Jonathan." She paused, feeling guiltier than ever. She tried to think straight. "Look, there's a big football rally tonight at Holliston Stadium. Why don't we go together?"

"A football rally?"

"Oh, I know it's just a college thing—kind of infantile," Stephanie said quickly. "But I—"

"I want to be wherever you are, Steph," Jonathan replied. "I'll meet you at the stadium gate at seven o'clock."

Stephanie hung up. When she looked up, she saw that Casey was staring at her.

"What's going on?" Casey stretched out on her

side, propping herself up on her elbow. She wiggled her freshly painted toes. "I thought you were crazy about Jonathan. But last night that wasn't your one and only true love you were kissing."

Stephanie pretended to be carefully choosing something to wear from her jam-packed closet. "Jonathan's fun," she said lightly. How could she tell Casey how she felt? She'd probably laugh. How could anyone take her feelings for Jonathan seriously after all the flirting she'd done since the beginning of the semester?

"Fun?"

"Don't be so naive, Casey," Stephanie blurted out, pulling on a black knit dress. "We're not *that* serious."

Casey looked stunned. "But you said . . ."

Stephanie pretended to check her hair in the mirror, then shoved her feet into flats and grabbed her makeup case again. "Jonathan's great," she said, giving herself a smile in the mirror, "but he's not the only male on the planet."

Casey's jaw dropped.

Stephanie moved toward the door, then turned around and gave Casey a sharp look. "Anyway, what happened last night with Mike is none of your business, Casey." Stephanie was out the door before Casey had a chance to reply.

Jake listened intently as the editor-in-chief of the *Wilder Times,* Gail Gardeski, explained the latest on a big Weston court case the newspaper was following.

"So, anyway," Gail was explaining, "this guy was convicted three years ago of robbing and sexually molesting three women in Weston, but his conviction was just thrown out, and he's getting a new trial. And—and it looks like he's going to be let out on bail."

Jake settled his cowboy boots up on his desk and took a sip of coffee from a cardboard cup. Floppy disks, tear sheets, felt pens and empty foam take-out containers littered his cubicle. A half-finished article flickered on his screen. "So now he'll be roaming the streets of Weston, huh?"

"Yeah," Gail said intently. Her expression was serious, as usual, and her black turtleneck made her look slimmer than ever. Not that Gail cared, Jake thought to himself. Gail was all business, and her life at the paper was everything to her. She was leaning against the tall file cabinet at the entrance to Jake's tiny work space, holding a printout of an article she'd been working on. "The guy found himself a smart lawyer who got hold of some new evidence."

"Sounds like a great story, Gail," Jake said.

Gail nodded. "It is. I'm really excited about it. I think this case is going to be major news in this area and maybe all over the country."

Jake swiveled back to face his computer screen. "Let me know if you need help."

"I'll need it." Gail popped her head back in

briefly. "I'm working on assignments for everyone."

Jake raked his fingers through his unruly hair and tried to concentrate on the story in front of him. But every time he started to write, a picture of Nancy's face kept popping up in his mind's eye. He grinned to himself. Beautiful, smart Nancy Drew. He loved the strawberry blond of her hair and the confident way she moved through life—always curious and ready for something new.

Still, Jake thought nervously, ever since their trip to River Heights she'd become distant. It had been great to meet her lawyer father, Carson Drew, his girlfriend, Avery, and the Drews' longtime housekeeper, Hannah Gruen. But Nancy had acted as if she were ready to pop out of her skin the entire weekend.

Jake sipped his coffee and played with buttons on his telephone. He just couldn't understand why Nancy would have a problem with Avery. Couldn't she see how happy the woman made her father? He'd been a widower for too long.

Making a fist, he slid his elbow out and rested his forehead on his knuckles. What it boiled down to was this: He'd felt like an outsider with her that weekend. And now that they were back at Wilder, the distance between them hadn't closed.

He dialed Nancy's number before he could think anymore. The football pep rally was that night, and they had a date. But Nancy wanted Bess, George, Will, and some others to join them.

Jake chewed his thumbnail while he waited for her to answer. He knew Nancy wanted to be with Bess, but Jake had hardly spent any time alone with Nancy since they got back from River Heights a week ago.

There was a beep, and then the sound of Nancy's recorded voice, asking the caller to leave a message.

Jake shook his head, and spoke into the phone. "Hi, Nan. It's Jake. Hey, why don't we get together before the pep rally tonight? Maybe grab a bite or something." Jake faltered, suddenly feeling self-conscious. "I'll drop by your room at six o'clock. We can go from there. See you then."

Chapter 4

"I tried calling the University Loan Servicing Center five or six times to find out why they hadn't paid my student bills after I'd sent them my loan money," George said worriedly.

"Are you sure you've been dialing the right number?" Nancy asked George, backing her Mustang out of the dorm parking lot.

George buckled her seat belt and crumpled the slip of paper in her hand. "I've checked the number a hundred times. The phone number and address of the place are right in the letter I received."

"No answer, huh?" Nancy asked. "Maybe they don't open until the afternoon."

George pushed her hair back. She had a strange and scary feeling that something was very wrong, despite Nancy's reassurances.

"The letter was on university letterhead?" Nancy asked.

"Yes," George replied, her anger building. "It was all very legit."

"We'll figure it out," Nancy said, trying to reassure her.

George bit her lip. "Thanks for taking me downtown."

"Okay, what's the address?" Nancy asked, driving off campus toward downtown Weston.

George smoothed out the slip of paper on her lap. "One Twenty-four Battery Street. Oh, and Pam also called the bursar's office to make sure *her* bills had been paid, since I was running into so many problems."

"You mean *she* signed over her loan check to University Loan Servicing Center, too?" Nancy looked worried.

"Yes," George replied grimly. "And the bursar's office gave her the same line. That her next semester's bills hadn't been paid. They were planning to call her this morning.

"Anyway, Pam had to get to class, so I told her I'd try to find out about our money." George shook her head, feeling foolish.

Nancy braked at an intersection and checked her map of downtown Weston. "Looks like the street is farther south," she murmured, turning left down a dismal street lined with boarded-up warehouses.

"How could I have been so stupid?" George

moaned as she stared out the car window. "This doesn't look good, Nan."

George could tell that Nancy was trying not to act worried. "Don't panic, George. Sometimes reputable office buildings are located on the fringes of districts like this."

George nodded, twisting her dark curls nervously as the car moved slowly down the street.

"I don't want to *think* about telling my parents if I can't find my money," George said.

"There's Battery Street," Nancy said. She turned the Mustang onto a wide street that was nearly empty, except for two pickup trucks parked in front of a tavern on the left. They scanned the storefronts until they reached 124 Battery.

George's heart sank as they got out of the car and approached the dingy office front. While Nancy tried the door, George peered in through the large front window. The office was deserted, except for a single desk with a phone. There was no sign for the University Loan Servicing Center on the building.

"It's locked, George." Nancy shook her head. George couldn't speak.

"Look," Nancy finally said. "Maybe we should drive around to see if we can find the ULSC sign on another building. There could have been a typo in that letter. It might be Twelve-forty Battery."

George looked at Nancy. "You don't have to

keep my hopes up. I've been scammed, Nancy. A bunch of jerks have stolen my money."

Nancy started to speak, then stopped and squinted at the doorjamb of the building entrance. "Look, George." Nancy pointed to a small sticker. "It's the name of the building's managing agent. Maybe we can find out more about who rented this place."

George dug into her purse and jotted down the address and phone number. "Acme Commercial Rentals," she said. "Doesn't sound promising."

"It's a start," Nancy said quietly, guiding George back to the car.

"Even if we do find out who rented this place," George wailed, slamming the door shut, "it doesn't mean Pam and I will ever get our money back!"

"Here we are," Montana was saying as she slid the large, warehouse door to the side. The blast of a loud electric guitar riff filled Ray's ears as he followed her in. "Cory knows we're coming, but we might have to wait a few minutes."

Ray nodded. Together they sat down on a pile of old crates at the edge of the room, and Ray carefully stowed his guitar case behind him.

Since meeting Montana at Java Joe's the night before, Ray'd been thinking a lot about the band she'd mentioned. Was it true he'd never be able to play with anyone but the Beat Poets? What was he going to do? Curl up and die because he'd had a few bad breaks in work and love? The more his thoughts churned, the more he was sure he was going to have to get his act together—fast. And this just might be the place to do it.

"Okay, Austin, I want to pick it up right here," a guy holding a bass guitar called out. He had a sturdy body and wavy, shoulder-length brown hair. A red bandanna was tied around his neck.

Montana waved at him. "That's Cory," she whispered to Ray. Cory nodded his head, smiled, and held up three fingers signaling it would be a few more minutes. "The drummer's name is Austin," she went on. "I don't like him as much as I like Cory, but he's really good, I think."

"Yeah," Ray agreed, watching Austin deliver a long set. Austin had a lean build and very shaggy, sandy hair. He wore a tight-fitting, striped T-shirt and black jeans.

"Okay," Cory called out with a flourish of his right hand after the last chord. He grinned at Montana and Ray. "Let's take five, Austin."

Ray watched as Cory hopped off the makeshift stage and approached. "Hey," Cory said, breathless. He bent his arm at the elbow and took Ray's hand in a vertical grip. A bead of sweat was trickling down the side of his face. "You must be Ray Johansson." He looked Ray right in the eye, nodding and smiling. "Beat Poets. Listened to you many times, man. Sorry to hear you broke up. You had something there."

"Yeah, well. That's the breaks," Ray replied.

Montana leaned forward. "Ray's still writing music. Right, Ray?"

Ray shrugged. "Put together a few tunes. Sure."

"Hey, Austin," Cory yelled over his shoulder. He settled onto a nearby packing box and reached into a cooler for a soda. Then he twisted off the top and took a long drink. "This is Ray. You know—Beat Poets."

Austin ambled down from the stage platform. His blue eyes were very light—almost transparent. "Hey, Ray. How's it going?"

Ray nodded. "Nice work."

"What we're trying to do right now is—" Cory began, but was interrupted by the loud noise of the warehouse door being thrown open with a bang.

Ray turned and watched as a girl with wild, jet-black hair and a pale face strode in, staring sourly at Austin and Cory. She was athletically slender, and her sleeveless black leather vest showed off her beautifully muscled arms. A heavy belt was looped through a pair of shredded, super-tight jeans, and her long earrings bobbed angrily as she walked.

Cory looked down and cleared his throat. "Hi, Karin."

Ray watched as the woman marched by. She said nothing but fixed an intense glare on Austin. She walked up to the stage, her boots echoing sharply on the wooden floorboards.

Montana leaned over and whispered in Ray's ear. "Karin used to be the band's lead vocalist. She played keyboards, too."

"I came to get my stuff," Karin said as she yanked an electrical plug from the wall at the back of the stage. She swiftly looped it between her thumb and elbow. Then she folded her keyboard, picked it up, and placed it on the metal cart she'd brought with her.

"Anyway, Ray . . ." Cory began again.

Ray stirred uncomfortably as Karin returned, marching right for him as if she was going to slug him.

"Uh—excuse me," Karin barked, and pointed to something just behind Ray. "You're sitting right in front of my amp."

Ray moved aside, exchanging glances with Montana.

With one swift movement, Karin yanked the cord of a large amp and picked it up, nearly hitting Ray in the head.

"Hey, Karin, watch it," Austin burst out, standing up. He stomped over to where she was already loading her cart and started arguing with her.

Ray and Montana looked on as Austin started to put a hand on Karin's arm, only to have her slap it away. There was a shout, and a moment later she was dragging her cart out the door, with Austin behind. They could hear muffled arguing on the sidewalk outside the warehouse.

"Just a second," Cory said. "I'll be right back." He followed the pair outside.

"Whew," Ray said, rubbing his hands up and

down the legs of his black jeans. "She is one angry chick."

Montana nodded. "Well, Karin and Austin used to be a very tight couple, and then they broke up."

Ray grimaced. "Man, I know what that's like."

"Oh, right," Montana said. "Anyway, Karin was—is—a really good musician. But Cory said that after the breakup she and Austin got crazy when they worked together. Argued constantly. Very bad situation."

Ray crossed his arms over his chest. "So, what happened?"

"The other band members, a lead guitarist and a male vocalist, couldn't handle it." Montana slid closer to Ray, crossing her leg so that it was almost touching his boot. "So they hooked up with a band in Chicago and left Cory and Austin stranded with only half a band. No keyboard. No lead guitar. And then Karin quit!"

The next moment Cory and Austin came back inside. Cory motioned Ray to join them on stage. "See you brought your guitar. Stick around. Jam with us for a while."

Looking flushed and happy, Montana gave Ray an eager smile and a thumbs-up sign. "Go for it."

Ray opened his guitar case and slung his instrument over his shoulder. Then he sauntered over and picked out a few short bars. Cory responded with a few of his own, and Ray felt the light, easy feeling come over him again. Music.

He stared at the door Karin had left through,

wondering what she'd sounded like with the band. Then he shook his head and smiled with relief. He was glad she was leaving the band. If he ended up playing with these guys, the last thing he needed was another soap opera in his life. What he wanted now was to have his own band again. To make music. To ride on its wave, pure and free.

"Hi, Bess." Bess listened to her answering machine in the dim light of her curtained dorm room. "It's Nancy. I just called to make sure you still want to come to the rally with us tonight. I think it'll be a lot of fun. Well, anyway, call me. Okay? 'Bye."

Bess slid farther down under her quilt, propping her biology notes up on her cast. She hated blowing off phone calls when she was right there. Especially since it was a close friend like Nancy. Not picking up the phone was almost like lying.

She peeled the wrapper off a candy bar and looked at her message machine. Now there were four blinks, she thought irritably. First Brian had called about the rally. Then George. Then Holly Thornton. And now Nancy. It seemed as if everyone was jostling to be her best baby-sitter.

"Besides," she muttered to herself, refocusing on her papers, "these notes are great. There's a shred of hope I'll pass biology now."

A few moments later Bess heard the key rattle and the door slowly opened. Out of the corner of her eye, she saw Leslie tiptoeing in.

"I'm not taking a nap," Bess said. "I'm studying."

Leslie beamed. "That's wonderful."

Bess cringed. "Yeah. I guess."

"I just had my last afternoon class," Leslie explained, dumping a tall pile of books.

Bess looked up at the ceiling, exasperated. "But you always go to the library after your last class."

Leslie gave her a secret smile and sat down on the bed next to her. "I know. But I brought you a present."

"What?" Bess tried to be patient.

"Two things." Leslie held out a bag she'd been hiding behind her back and grinned. "One pint of your favorite Jamaica Walnut Swirl ice cream."

Bess smiled and took the bag. Then she sat up on the bed and stacked her bio notes on her knees. "Thanks, Les. What else?"

"More study sheets," Leslie said, slipping her an envelope. "I stopped by the bio department and got them. They're new."

"Thanks." Bess sighed. She'd already asked Ginny Yuen to tutor her in biology, so she didn't really need the bio notes. But she didn't want to hurt Leslie's feelings by not taking them.

"Well," Leslie said briskly, standing up. "Is everything okay?"

Bess wanted to scream, but she reminded herself to keep calm. Flipping out would only put Leslie and the others on super red alert. "Yes—yes, everything's just fine," she lied.

"Did you call that counselor?" Leslie asked casually.

"Yes, I did," Bess replied, flipping through the bio notes. "I'm going to see her tomorrow."

"Great," Leslie said, giving her a happy smile.

Bess looked at her watch, hoping Leslie would finally get the message and leave her in peace. "Aren't you going to the pep rally?"

"Yes." Leslie got up and opened her closet, eyeing her wardrobe. "You are, too, aren't you? Everybody wants to see you."

Bess hunkered down under her quilt. "Not me. I'm going to take this opportunity to study these lovely bio notes you gave me."

Leslie swiveled around, surprised. "You are? Well, let me stay and help you. I know all of that stuff backward and forward."

Bess opened her mouth to say something, but no words came out. She watched in horror as Leslie eagerly settled into her desk and gave her a thumbs-up sign. Bess was completely and totally stuck with study sheets *and* Leslie. This wasn't help. This was torture!

Chapter 5

"I can't believe that was your first time jamming together," Montana said happily. "You and Cory and Austin were awesome."

Ray took a large bite of pizza, chewed, and gave a cheerful shrug. "Sometimes it works. Sometimes it doesn't, I guess."

Montana leaned across her plate with an eager expression. "Are you kidding? How can you be so laid back? It was fantastic."

Ray grinned at her, then looked at the busy crowd packing the inside of the pizza parlor. Montana was right, of course. Inside he was kicking and screaming with joy, but he was still making himself hold back a little. It was almost too good to be true. This afternoon he had really clicked with Cory and Austin, and they'd ended up jamming until dark.

"What I'm trying to say," Montana explained, "is that the combination seemed to work. Cory's bass was—"

"We didn't even have an arrangement," Ray interrupted. "It was intuitive. The whole thing."

"Cory's playing was . . ." Montana began again.

Ray nodded before she could finish her sentence. "Aggressive. It's an aggressive attitude. It's a kind of jackhammer groove he has that gets me going."

"Yeah," Montana echoed back.

Ray felt his head spinning with excitement. "I felt like I was coming into my own with the vocals. And with Cory and Austin backing me up, I almost felt as if I could play rhythm and lead at the same time. Like I was playing two guitars at the same time."

Montana nodded, sipping her soda, then setting it down. "I know what you mean."

Ray took a breath and leaned back in his chair. He smiled at Montana, suddenly grateful. "Thanks, by the way."

Montana's face lit up. "You're welcome."

Ray narrowed his eyes. "What made you so sure we'd hit it off?"

Montana gave him a mysterious look. "Intuition."

Ray laughed. Maybe she was right. His gut instinct told him that he was finding his energy again. Cory and Austin had even played around with Ray's own tunes, and they'd looked impressed. Tomorrow they were meeting for another session.

"Sometimes that's what the most important things in life boil down to," Montana said. She was studying him with a curious expression.

"Boil down to?"

"Intuition," Montana said simply. "That's how I felt the first time I did the radio talk show with Kara and Nikki." She covered her laugh with her hand. "We were filling in for someone who'd picked a really dull student government topic and—"

Ray laughed. "I heard about that."

"Oh, no!"

Ray pointed teasingly at Montana. "You asked your listeners what they looked for in their perfect guy—or girl, right?"

Montana nodded. "*Everyone* wanted to talk. We had callers coming out of our ears. The show was a hit and now we're regulars." She shook her head happily. "But it wasn't because we followed the rules."

"Yeah," Ray said, suddenly thoughtful. "You followed your gut instincts."

"Yep." Montana peeled off another slice of pizza and bit into it.

Music began to flood out of the restaurant jukebox, and Ray relaxed in his seat. Life was feeling a whole lot better again. Montana was fun, and he was grateful to her for pulling him out of the dark funk he'd been in. He still missed Ginny—sometimes he missed her so much his insides ached. He definitely wasn't ready for another relationship yet. But it felt good right now to be with a friend who just happened to be a girl.

He felt his heart speed up and the darkness inside of him lift. He felt as if he was starting to put his life back together.

Nancy put on a fresh blouse and tucked it into her jeans. Peering into her dorm mirror, she gave her hair a quick brush and dabbed on a little lipstick. In five minutes she was supposed to meet Jake at the dorm entrance to go to the big football rally.

"That will have to do," she muttered to herself, trying not to knock over the dozen or so herbal lotion bottles her roommate, Kara, had left out.

It was the first minute Nancy had been able to catch her breath all day. She'd had an early class, followed by her trip to the vacant student loan center with George. After that, there had been classes, a couple of intense study hours in the library, followed by a staff meeting down at the *Times* newsroom.

Turning around to search for her purse, Nancy noticed the blinking red light on her answering machine, and reached over to give it a punch.

"Hi, Nancy," she heard her father's voice. Nancy frowned briefly. Her father, Carson Drew, a normally energetic River Heights lawyer, sounded weary. "This is Dad. Sure loved seeing you and Jake last weekend. Nancy, I feel we really need to talk, and I was hoping we could do it before too long. Try to give me a call when you're free, okay? Bye, bye."

Nancy erased the message and made a mental note to call him back. Then she slipped a jacket out of her closet and put it on, aware of the heavy feeling her dad's message had given her. He'd sounded pretty anxious to talk to her, and she knew why.

Things hadn't gone well between Avery and her. Nancy had felt pushed out of her own home, and her father hadn't understood. He'd even been angry with her after an uncomfortable scene Nancy had had with Avery at breakfast one morning.

Still too confused to talk to her father, Nancy decided to put off calling him back. She needed to free herself up for a few hours.

After all, Nancy decided, if I think too hard about George's money troubles, Bess's recovery, and Dad's new relationship, I'll be fried. There won't be anything left for me or Jake.

She checked her watch quickly and dashed out the door. When she got to the lobby, she could see Jake waiting outside. They would have to go straight to the stadium and skip dinner. It was seven already.

"Hi," she called.

Jake smiled as she walked up. "You look breathless."

Nancy took in Jake's new denim shirt and faded jeans. His brown hair was still wet and combed back from a shower, revealing his deep, brown eyes and the fine features of his face. There was a kind of boyish, sexy intelligence in his smile that always made her a little weak in the knees. And right now, just looking at him made Nancy feel as if everything in her life was going to work out.

"Maybe you just take my breath away," Nancy said quietly, only half joking.

Jake gave her a surprised look, which melted into a smile. They walked down the front steps of the dorm and headed across the leafy campus toward the stadium. "Whoa. Where did that come from?"

Nancy smiled back at him, took a deep breath, and felt all of the problems of the day slip away. Just walking across the grass with Jake's hand in hers made everything else seem very distant and unimportant.

The crowds thickened as they approached Holliston Stadium. The rally would be starting in only a few minutes, but Nancy didn't feel like hurrying.

"Come here," Jake said gently, and Nancy could tell he was sensing her mood. He steered her toward a secluded spot behind one of the maples surrounding the stadium. Then he slipped his arms around her waist and looked deep into her eyes. "Everything okay?"

Nancy tensed a little. She wanted to be with Jake, but she didn't want to get involved in a serious talk. Her feelings were too jumbled at the moment for that. Instead, she kissed him gently on the lips and smiled. "Sure."

"You're not still angry about your dad and Avery . . ." Jake began to ask.

Nancy pulled away. "I've got a lot going on right now," she faltered. "You know? With Bess, and now George is having problems. And there are classes and articles for the newspaper."

Jake frowned. "I know but—"

"I've been a little edgy," Nancy admitted. "And maybe my dad's new life with Avery is connected to that, Jake," she said quickly. "But I don't want to think about that right now. I just want to mellow out tonight. Please try to understand."

Jake focused on the toe of his cowboy boot.

Nancy touched the side of his face. "Let's go in there and have a good time."

Jake nuzzled the side of her neck, then smiled. "I've been a mess lately, too. Forget it."

Nancy felt her heart expand. Jake's hands were on her shoulders, gently turning her face to his. Then, in the growing darkness, he gave her a long, sweet kiss. And in that moment she remembered how much they meant to each other and how much they still had to learn about each other. The problems they'd had on their trip to River Heights were just a minor setback. Things were bound to work out—just as they had before.

Stephanie stood at the ivy-covered entrance to Holliston Stadium, straining for a glimpse of Jonathan's chestnut brown hair in the crowd. The noisy, banner-waving football fans jostled her against the wall, but Stephanie held fast. She would wait for Jonathan as long as it took. Casey had promised to save a pair of seats for them.

"Everything will be perfect tonight," Stephanie murmured to herself, hopping on her toes to see over the crush of bodies. She looked down at Jonathan's friendship ring and the black jumpsuit she was wearing—his favorite.

Stephanie shivered, remembering her encounter with Mike at the Underground party the night before. Confusion and guilt began to overcome her.

"This is ridiculous," Stephanie whispered to herself. "What was I doing with Mike when I have Jonathan?"

Stephanie's thoughts drifted back to high school, where she'd had lots of dates and attention, but few guys she really cared about. Now she'd fallen in love, and it felt like a dream come true. Or was it?

Stephanie kept searching the faces in the crowd for Jonathan's, suddenly desperate to see him, just so she could make him real again. Last night, when she'd been with Mike, she'd almost convinced herself that Jonathan hadn't really meant it when he said he loved her.

"Looking for someone?" she heard a masculine voice say in a way that made her feel scared and excited at the same time. But it wasn't Jonathan's voice. It was Mike's.

"Stephanie?" Mike touched her arm.

Stephanie bit her lip, staring at his incredible smile. There was something adorable about the way his dark hair curled around his forehead.

Mike was staring at her. "You all by yourself?" he asked.

Stephanie looked Mike in the eye and steadied herself. "Not for long."

"Mmm," Mike went on, moving closer. "Waiting for a girlfriend?"

"Wouldn't you like to know," Stephanie teased back.

"Come here," Mike said into her ear, taking her hand and motioning toward a nearby concrete wall with a line of juniper trees in front of it.

Stephanie tried to think. She should get rid of Mike, and fast. But his aftershave smelled so good, and she couldn't get the taste of his kisses from the night before out of her mind. Stephanie quickly decided to use this opportunity to tell him the truth about her steady boyfriend.

"You've got exactly thirty seconds," Stephanie said, allowing herself to be pulled into the privacy of the trees. "Look," she began, reaching both hands up and straightening Mike's collar. "I'm here with someone. So you need to go away, and . . ."

Before she could finish, however, Mike had pulled her close and was pressing her to his broad chest. A moment later his lips were on hers, and she felt her resolve sag.

"Stephanie," he murmured, moving his hands down her back.

She opened her mouth to explain, but Mike quickly dropped his lips to hers again. Instinctively, she pressed forward and wrapped her arms around his neck. After all, Stephanie thought, Mike was an amazingly good kisser.

Finally Mike broke away and Stephanie gasped for breath. One of his hands was pressed firmly against the wall, pinning her. "Sit with me at the rally?" Mike asked her, leaning in again to kiss her neck.

She started to protest, realizing what she'd just done. But Mike's body was so irresistible. It was impossible for her to pull away!

"Knock it off," Stephanie said, and pulled back a little. Her whole body was tingling with his kisses. Taking one long fingernail, she stroked the underside of his chin. "I'm not here at your beck and call, you know."

Mike pretended to look around, then grinned at her. "Looks like you are to me."

Stephanie started to laugh but stopped suddenly when she heard a voice calling for her.

"What's wrong?" Mike said.

Panicked, Stephanie shoved him away.

"Stephanie?" she heard Jonathan's voice in the crowd. She could tell he was only a few feet away, on the other side of the trees.

"Oh, no," Stephanie cried as she spun around and smoothed her hair. The shock of hearing

Jonathan while she was so near to Mike sent her into emotional overload.

"But, baby . . ." she heard Mike's voice trailing off behind her as she broke away and dashed back toward the entrance to the stadium. Desperately, she ran her finger around the outside of her lipline, trying to make sure her lipstick wasn't smudged. A second later she saw him. Jonathan was standing next to Casey at the entrance, craning his neck in the opposite direction.

Please don't turn around, Stephanie prayed to herself, hoping he wouldn't see Mike.

Coming up behind him, Stephanie pressed her hands over Jonathan's eyes. "Guess who?" she said, trying to control her nervous voice.

Jonathan turned around and gave her a beautiful smile. He was only wearing a heavy sweatshirt and jeans, but he looked better than anything she'd ever laid eyes on. Quickly, she kissed him, hoping he wouldn't smell Mike's aftershave or notice how disheveled she looked.

"Steph," Jonathan said with a tender look. "Where were you? I ran into Casey, and we've been searching all over for you."

Stephanie forced herself not to scan the crowd for Mike, but she thought she detected the suspicion in Casey's eyes. "Sorry. I just ran into someone," Stephanie murmured in Jonathan's ear. "Let's find our seats."

"Okay," Jonathan agreed, wrapping his arm around her waist.

But an instant later Stephanie caught a glimpse

of Casey's face and realized she had spotted Mike emerging from their hiding place. Slowly, Casey turned toward Stephanie, and as they walked with Jonathan to their seats, Stephanie could see Casey's dark, accusing look.

"Give me an *N,*" the Wilder cheerleader was screaming into a megaphone.

George looked happily over at Will, Pam, and Jamal as they joined in the cheer with the rest of the crowd in Holliston Stadium.

She took in big gulps of evening air and reached around Will's waist. Coming to the rally was the best thing she could have done tonight, George realized. She'd been devastated that afternoon when she found the University Loan Servicing Center office abandoned. Her college money for next semester—where was it?

George felt tears of frustration and anger pressing against the back of her eyes and cheered even louder, suddenly grateful for the good friends surrounding her in the stands. At least she had them, no matter what happened. The only one missing, though, was Bess. That worried George, since she and Nancy had both been trying to reach her all day.

"And noooooowwwwww, Norsemen fans!" the stadium announcer suddenly yelled. "I'd like you to give a warm welcome to our very own team. Wilder's finest, the Norsemen!"

George recognized Eileen's boyfriend, Emmet Lehman, as he sped onto the field with the rest of his squad. Suddenly the lump of anger and sadness in George's throat melted away.

"Emmet!" Eileen waved a big posterboard sign wildly at the field, her face radiant. George heard a laugh and looked over to see Nancy pointing at Eileen's sign and applauding. She seemed to be having a great time, cheering in the crisp air with Jake at her side.

"Take one, George," Pam was calling out, passing her a blue-and-white flag with a large Norseman *N*. She and Jamal were holding their flags up together, fluttering them against the darkening sky.

"Hey, everyone," Eileen yelled to the group as Emmet bounded back up into the stands. "Did you hear the good news about Emmet?"

"What's up?" George asked.

"Well"—Eileen grinned—"tell them, Emmet."

"Eileen's talking about my brother Jason's new club downtown," Emmet said. "Looks like I'll be working there part-time, starting this week."

"Cool," George cried, as everyone excitedly agreed.

Emmet grinned. "I'm just helping out on the business end."

"We'll need free club passes, Emmet," Pam teased.

The group looked out at the field again as the cheerleaders burst back onto the field. Nancy stood up to squeeze in next to George and Pam on the bleachers.

"How's it going?" she asked them over the

roar of the crowd. "Any more news about your loan money?" George shook her head. "Eileen's been stung, too. She called the bursar's office and checked on *her* bills."

Nancy's blue eyes widened. "They hadn't been paid either?"

"Nope," Pam said.

"Did the bursar's office offer to help?" Nancy asked. "They must realize that something's up. After all, at least three people have reported the problem—and you've all mentioned the University Loan Servicing Center specifically."

Pam shook her head. "She said the bursar's office actually gave her a bad time about it."

Nancy's eyebrows lifted.

George cast a glance toward Eileen and Emmet. "Eileen told me she was going to put it out of her mind tonight and try to have fun."

Pam's dark eyes were worried. "I was talking to a guy in my political science class who had the same thing happen to him."

"He got the same letter recommending ULSC on the university's letterhead?" George asked, surprised.

"Yep," Pam answered. "He sent his loan check to them—"

"And found out his bills are still unpaid," George finished her sentence. "I wonder how many people got the letter?"

"Since he works there part-time, Jamal is on pretty good terms with the people at the student loan office," Pam said. "So he promised to go down there with me tomorrow morning to try to iron things out."

"I want to go, too," George said. "I don't have any classes before lunch."

"Everything's going to be fine, George," Will whispered in her ear, slipping a strong arm around her waist.

George turned and looked up at his comforting, dark eyes and, at least for a moment, she felt the weight of the world disappear.

Chapter 6

"Ginny! Turn the alarm off!"

Ginny Yuen slowly opened her eyes. She heard the ringing of her alarm, but it had seemed so far away.

"Ginny?" she could hear her roommate, Liz Bader, grumbling across the room.

Ginny reached for the clock and shut it off. Then she collapsed back on her pillow.

"What's with you?" Liz asked, getting out of bed.

"I'm just a little tired," Ginny confessed, rubbing her eyes. "Took me a long time to fall asleep last night."

"Mmmm." Liz said as she put on a bathrobe. "You've got something on your mind. And his name begins with the letter *R.*"

Ginny looked up with a half smile. "Your New York City street smarts are kicking in."

"Well?" Liz put her hand on her hip.

Ginny sat up in bed, then flopped back down again. "Okay. It's Ray."

"You miss him, don't you?" Liz asked.

Ginny nodded. "Yeah. I do."

Liz rummaged through a drawer, then drew out a bottle of shampoo and a purple towel. "Okay. What brought this on?"

"I saw him last night at the football rally," Ginny confessed. "With someone else."

Liz's expression turned sympathetic. "Oh. That must have been a drag."

Ginny felt a lump in her throat. "You bet."

"Who was it?" Liz asked gently.

Ginny gulped. "Montana Smith. I just didn't think I'd mind that much or that I . . ."

Liz's eyebrows shot up. "Montana?"

"Yes," Ginny replied, trying to throw off the mood. She got up and padded across the room toward her own closet. "Blond, newly famous radio talk-show host Montana Smith."

"She doesn't waste any time," Liz drawled, moving toward the door with her shower things under her arm.

"Yeah," Ginny said, sad and guilty at the same time. After all, she'd been to the rally, too, with Frank Chung. And even if she wasn't that serious about Frank, she *had* been dating him. She couldn't expect a guy like Ray to be a hermit for the rest of his life.

"Come on, Ginny," Liz protested, sticking her head back through the door just before she closed it. "I mean, we're talking about Montana Smith, airhead extraordinaire. You are a beautiful, smart, kind person who's got a lot going for her. Don't let someone like Montana make you jealous."

Ginny sighed as Liz shut the door. Then she looked at herself in the mirror and dragged her brush through her long, dark hair. "Am I jealous of Montana?" she said softly to herself. "Yes, I am. Once I had Ray's heart all to myself, and now I think she's got a piece of it."

Nancy hurried across the Mall on her way to her first class. Passing by some very tired-looking girls and then a group of bleary-eyed Norsemen football players sipping coffee out of cardboard cups, Nancy smiled to herself. Everyone seemed pretty clouded over. It had been a wild night after the tumultuous rally at Holliston Stadium. The entire campus had been peppered with parties from the frat houses, to the dorms, to the off-campus housing.

"Nancy, hi!" she heard someone calling behind her.

Nancy turned and saw Brian Daglian running up. "Hey, Brian."

Brian panted as he slowed down beside her. He had a worried look on his face. "Have you seen Bess lately?"

"No," Nancy answered. "I haven't seen her since Sunday night at the Underground."

Brian rubbed the back of his neck and looked

down. "Neither have I. We were supposed to have lunch yesterday, but she canceled. Since then, she hasn't returned any of my messages."

Nancy nodded. "She hasn't returned my calls either."

"I'm worried," Brian said. "It's not like Bess."

"We have to give her a little time, I think."

"But she doesn't have to suffer through this all by herself," Brian blurted out. "She has people who love her and want to help."

"I know," Nancy answered, acutely aware of how many people were also hurting from Paul Cody's death and Bess's pain. The effects of the tragedy were like ripples on the surface of a pond—widening by the hour.

Brian gave Nancy a frustrated look. "I wish *she* knew."

"Maybe we're all giving her a lot of good advice she can't take right now," Nancy replied.

"Yeah. I hear you," Brian said doubtfully. "But I still would like to know if she's okay."

"George has been trying to reach Bess, too," Nancy told him. "She's having some major problems of her own. But all she gets is Bess's answering machine."

Brian shook his head. "Bummer. Bess would want to talk to George if she knew George was having a problem."

Nancy nodded. "I agree, but Bess is trying really hard to catch up with her classes. I can see why she feels she needs time alone right now."

Brian was doubtful. "Sorry, Nancy. I don't feel better."

"Look," Nancy said. "Let's both track her down after our classes. One of us is bound to find her."

"Deal," Brian agreed. "Let's snag her and pin her to the ground."

Nancy smiled as they walked through the entrance to Graves Hall along with the surging student crowd.

"What's going on with George?" Brian called out. "Is she okay?"

Nancy grimaced, grabbed his elbow and led him toward the staircase. "Walk with me and I'll tell you about it. It's pretty serious. And if she doesn't get to the bottom of it, George may not be at Wilder next semester."

"The student loan office handles a lot of paperwork every day, especially at this time of year," Jamal was explaining. "Everyone's sending in money for next semester."

"Sounds pretty hectic," George said, tightening the grip on her backpack. She followed Eileen, Pam, and Jamal up the granite front steps of the university administration building. Since Jamal worked there part-time, George hoped he could straighten out the loan mess for all of them.

"There's no way this isn't a gigantic misunderstanding," Eileen said confidently. "Things like this don't happen."

"Yeah," Pam agreed. "Thousands of dollars in tuition money don't just fly away into thin air."

Jamal led the way through the building's heavy glass door, looking hopeful. "Well, Marsha Sorenson is the assistant in the front office, and she knows just about everything there is to know about student loans."

As the foursome headed down a long hall, George spotted the large sign for the student loan office near the end of the corridor. "Thanks for doing this, Jamal." George patted his broad shoulder as they walked in.

"No problem," Jamal said. "Life has a funny way of sneaking up on you if you don't stay on your toes."

"With a little help from our friends," Eileen said, "we'll have the university on its knees, begging for our forgiveness."

George looked up as a tired-looking, middle-aged woman walked into the front office, intently studying a clipboard.

"Marsha?" Jamal said politely.

The woman's head jerked up, and she gave Jamal a curt smile. "Oh, hello, Jamal. You working today?" Then she sat down, stuck a pencil between her teeth, and yanked open a file cabinet next to her desk.

George, Eileen, and Pam exchanged glances. The woman appeared to be totally ignoring them.

"No, I'm not. Actually, Marsha," Jamal continued, "I'm trying to help some friends of mine with a serious problem."

Sitting back in her office chair, Marsha gave a dismal sigh. "Jamal. If your friends need help, they'll have to make an appointment first."

"Marsha," Jamal broke in, the jawbone in his tawny face tightening. "I just need a minute of your time. This is very impor—"

"We can't wait," Eileen said. "This is an emergency."

Marsha shot her an impatient glance.

"Look, Marsha," Jamal said calmly, "if you're busy, I'd like to check in with Ruth Hill. I'm sure it won't take more than—"

Marsha's eyes flashed with anger. "Mrs. Hill is on the phone and she is booked solid with appointments all day long," she snapped.

George stirred uncomfortably. What was this woman's problem?

"Well, then," Jamal said coolly, firmly guiding George, Pam, and Eileen toward a door at the other end of the room. "I'll just poke my old head through the door and say hello."

"Wait a min—" Marsha began to protest just as Jamal opened a door that read Ruth Hill—Director, Wilder Student Loan Office.

"Mrs. Hill!" George heard Jamal's cheerful greeting.

Quickly the three girls filed into a large, carpeted room with an oak desk. Behind the desk stood a trim woman in a red suit, just hanging up the phone and busily jotting something down on a notepad. She gave a broad smile, walked around the desk, and extended her hand.

"Jamal," she said warmly, shaking his hand. "I thought you worked late in the afternoon. Can't stay away?"

Relief surged through George's veins just looking at Mrs. Hill's reasonable face and crisp salt-and-pepper hair. She looked like the kind of woman who was used to solving problems—and would definitely be able to solve theirs.

Jamal cleared this throat as Mrs. Hill looked at them expectantly. "Mrs. Hill, I hope you don't mind this intrusion. . . ."

"Oh, for goodness' sake, Jamal," Mrs. Hill protested, extending her hand to George.

"These are my friends George Fayne, Eileen O'Connor, and Pam Miller," Jamal went on seriously. "I have a feeling you'll be interested in what they have to say."

Mrs. Hill motioned for everyone to sit, then perched on the edge of her desk. "Please. Tell me what's the matter," she said politely. "I have a few moments before my next meeting."

George felt her courage mounting and spoke up. "Two weeks ago, Mrs. Hill, I received a letter from this office recommending that I use a company called the University Loan Servicing Center."

Mrs. Hill opened her mouth to speak, but closed it again and narrowed her eyes—intent on what George was saying.

"Anyway," George continued, "the letter said we could now mail our checks to the ULSC, instead of the Wilder Student Loan Office. . . ."

"And they would take care of paying our student expenses covered by the loans," Pam broke in, leaning forward.

Doubt flickered in Mrs. Hill's eyes, and George noticed she was frowning suspiciously. "So, you sent your loan money to this organization?" Mrs. Hill asked.

George bit her lip. "Yes."

"But none of our bills have been paid," Eileen blurted.

"We tracked down the ULSC office," George said nervously. "Or—the address where we'd sent our money. But it was deserted."

There was a long silence as Mrs. Hill walked slowly around her desk.

Jamal stirred in his chair. "So, as you can see, my friends are in some real trouble."

"And since the letter was sent to us on official Wilder stationery—" Pam began lamely.

"But we did not send out any letters recommending this service," Mrs. Hill said abruptly, giving Pam a sharp look.

George had a sinking feeling in her stomach, suddenly noticing that Mrs. Hill's eyes were a very cold shade of gray.

Jamal sat up rigidly in his chair. "Well, of course, that's what we've come to realize, Mrs. Hill. That's why we're here. It looks as if my friends have been the victims of some kind of fraud, to put it bluntly."

Mrs. Hill seemed to be unmoved.

"Scammed," Jamal repeated, "by someone

using the university's name. Come on, this has got to be important to you, too."

George took a copy of the letter out of her backpack and slipped it in front of Mrs. Hill. The woman eyed it briefly without touching it.

"Mrs. Hill?" Pam tried to prompt her. "Is there anything you can do to help us?"

George felt ill. Mrs. Hill looked about as sympathetic as a statue. "I have never heard of the University Loan Servicing Center," Mrs. Hill said.

"Yes, but—" Jamal tried to break in.

"Furthermore," Mrs. Hill interrupted, pointing at him, "as an employee here, Jamal, you must realize that we don't make deals with *any* outside parties to handle student education funds."

Jamal's mouth tightened, and George could barely breathe. They had come for help, and now the university was refusing to listen.

"So what are we going to do?" Eileen asked angrily. "How are we going to get our money back?"

Mrs. Hill gave everyone a long, hard stare. "I find some of your facts very suspicious."

"What?" George asked, bristling with anger.

"First, I find it strange that no other students have come forward," Mrs. Hill said. "Secondly, I find it very odd that someone running a scam would target only three students—students who, in fact, know one another," Mrs. Hill said, casting a look toward George. "You are all friends, I take it?"

George wanted to cry. Instead, she lifted her chin up. "Yes, we are friends, Mrs. Hill."

Pam spoke up quickly. "But there's a guy I barely know in my political theory class, too, who—"

"Young lady," Mrs. Hill interrupted, "Wilder University keeps in touch with university student loan offices all over the country. . . ."

"Mrs. Hill—" Jamal tried to break in.

"And we've learned that fraud is increasing at an alarming rate," she went on. "We've found that students have cheated the system using a number of ways in order to receive more money than they actually need for college expenses. Or, sometimes, even to skip college altogether and just take the money."

"What are you implying?" Eileen asked indignantly.

George's mouth dropped open. Mrs. Hill was being more than suspicious.

"We have reports of other scammers who've played the part of the victim," Mrs. Hill continued. "Students who claim their money was stolen, then expect the university to make up the difference, thus doubling their—"

"Mrs. Hill!" Jamal exclaimed, standing up. "You are accusing my friends of fraud."

"It happens all the time," she replied coolly.

"How dare you?" George snapped, standing up with Jamal. "We came to you for help!"

Jamal crossed his arms over his chest. "And

how do you think they managed to pull off this amazing fraud?"

Mrs. Hill narrowed her eyes. "It could have been done easily, as you know, Jamal. You work here. Our office stationery is out for anyone to use."

"This is bizarre!" Eileen exclaimed.

"Obviously I'm not saying that *you* did these things," Mrs. Hill said slowly. "I just want you to be aware. We know of some students at other universities who've *pretended* to be victims of scams. But, of course, they'd made up their stories and had actually kept the money."

"But what are we supposed to do?" George asked angrily. "Just drop out of school because we've been ripped off and you won't believe us?"

Mrs. Hill's expression turned to stone. "Don't expect us to give you a break on your tuition."

There was a hush, and George thought she could hear her heart beat.

Mrs. Hill stood up abruptly. "I want you to know that I'll be making a full report of this incident to the dean's office. And I assure you, we will be in touch with you soon."

George, Jamal, Eileen, and Pam rose, speechless. George couldn't believe what she'd just heard. The university loan office actually suspected *them* of fraud? George suddenly had another thought that almost made her knees buckle. If the university could somehow prove they committed fraud, then paying for next semester would be the least of their problems. They could be in serious trouble with the law!

Chapter 7

Bess shut her notebook and stuffed it briskly into her bookbag as her psych professor concluded his lecture.

Most of the students crowded noisily into the lecture hall aisles, while a few others cornered the professor next to his lectern. All Bess wanted to do was hurry back to her dorm so she could catch up on her reading. She prayed there wouldn't be any more messages on her answering machine.

"Is this yours?" A girl from her dorm approached her, holding out a pen.

Bess looked at her sad, sympathetic expression and stirred uncomfortably. There was that look again. The same painful look she got from nearly everyone these days. "Thanks," Bess said lightly, taking the pen.

"You're welcome," the girl said, biting her lip and turning to join her friends in the aisle.

Bess heard whispering behind her, and when she turned around, a group of girls she knew from another sorority were suddenly silent.

"Hi, Bess," one girl said in a tiny voice.

"Hi," Bess answered, yanking her bookbag onto her shoulder and storming out of the lecture hall. It was the same everywhere. Conversations that turned silent. Eyes that dropped. Bess understood that it was hard for some people to know what to say. But the atmosphere was beginning to suffocate her.

Hurrying out of the building's side entrance, Bess took the long route back to her dorm through the faculty parking lot, the cafeteria's maintenance driveway, then a secluded path to the back entrance of Jamison Hall.

Bess began to breathe easier once she reached her dorm. Leslie had lab every Tuesday afternoon, so Bess knew she'd have the room to herself. She longed for solitude now—just as she used to long for Paul and his gentle touch.

Once she reached her floor, however, her heart sank. Brian was standing next to her door.

"Hi, Bess," he said quietly. "I was hoping I'd find you."

Bess gritted her teeth and stuck her key into the lock. "Hi, there." She stretched her mouth into a smile. Having a few minutes to herself without sympathetic friends was too much to hope for. "Everything going okay?" Brian wanted to know, following her in through the door.

"Sure," Bess said casually, tossing her bookbag on the bed. "Everything's great."

Brian gave her a small smile, but Bess knew he wasn't buying into her upbeat act. Brian was aware she was in pain, and he wanted her to open up. But how could she tell him that something inside her still clamped shut when she tried to talk about Paul? It was impossible. Her feelings were too confused.

"What's wrong?" Brian asked simply. "Everyone's trying to reach you. You're not returning phone messages. No one could find you at the rally last night."

"I'm okay," Bess said, trying to reassure him. "I just need some time to myself."

Brian studied his toes, not convinced.

"Look," Bess argued, unzipping her bookbag. "I'll feel a lot better about everything once I get my classwork under control, Brian. I know that doesn't sound like me, but it's true. I just need to feel—like I have things *under control.*"

Brian opened his mouth to say something, then appeared to change his mind. "Actually, I've come bearing good news."

"I could use some good news," Bess said with a smile.

"I'm offering my services to help you prepare your audition for Jeanne Glasseburg," Brian said.

Bess's ears pricked up. Jeanne Glasseburg was a prominent New York director hired to teach an invitation-only, one-time acting class at Wilder the next semester. Casey Fontaine and Brian had been invited to attend after Ms. Glasseburg saw their work in a performance of one-act plays. But the one-acts had been right after Bess's motorcycle accident with Paul, and Bess had been forced to drop out of the plays. Ms. Glasseburg had offered Bess a chance to audition privately for the class when she had recuperated from the accident.

"Oh," Bess said. "I haven't even thought about my audition."

"Well," Brian said, stepping closer, "you'd better. She's going back to New York."

Bess gasped. "When?"

"Next week."

Bess drew her hands up to her face and shook her head. "I can't be ready with something that soon."

"You'll be great," Brian assured her.

Bess's heart was sinking into her knees. "It's too much, Brian. It's just too much."

"Casey and I will help," Brian said cheerfully.

Bess folded her arms over her chest and looked out the window. "Everything all at once. It's too much, Brian."

Brian cleared his throat. "Speaking of people with too much to handle. It's terrible about George, isn't it?"

Bess whirled around. "What?"

"You haven't talked to her?" Brian asked. "You didn't hear what happened?"

Bess's jaw dropped. "N-no. She called, but I didn't return . . . I mean, I thought she just wanted to . . ."

"Talk about your problems?" Brian filled in.

Bess sat down, flooded with guilt. "What happened, Brian?"

"Someone may have scammed away all of George's student loan money," Brian explained.

"What?"

"George, Pam Miller, and Eileen O'Connor all got letters on university stationery recommending that they sign over their loan checks to some business that would distribute their funds to all the appropriate departments," Brian explained. "It sounded pretty routine, but now they've discovered that someone probably stole the stationery and made up a sham company. Nancy and George went out yesterday to the office address that was given in the letter, and the office was deserted."

"Poor George," Bess said. "This is terrible."

"I know," Brian said.

Bess sprang up and stared out the window into the trees and walkways below. George was in serious trouble, and she didn't even know it. The thought brought a lump to her throat. She'd been so wrapped up in her own problems that she'd practically abandoned one of the people she loved most.

"Come on," Nancy called out as George ran down the front steps of her dorm.

"Did you call the Acme Commercial Rentals office?" George gasped, jumping into the passenger seat and slamming the door.

Nancy stepped on the accelerator and headed downtown toward the deserted storefront they'd visited the day before. "Yes. A guy named Mr. Micelli agreed to meet me there, but he told me to hurry."

George stared. "What did you say to him?"

"I told him I was interested in renting some office space," Nancy said.

George clenched her jaw. "This is beginning to sound like a bad movie—with me as the star."

"Calm down," Nancy replied. "We might be able to find out something from this guy."

After George's disastrous meeting in the student loan office that morning, she'd called Nancy for help. Nancy had suggested they see the rental agent of the deserted building.

"But the office is already rented, isn't it?" George suddenly asked. "Why would Mr. Micelli come dashing out to meet us if someone's already paying for it?"

Nancy gave George a sideways smile. "He made it pretty clear he'd happily kick out his current tenant if we could pay him more."

"He sounds like a total sleazebag," George moaned.

"But at least he's willing to meet with us right away," Nancy pointed out. "And we might come up with something when we're in the office."

"Names, files, anything," George agreed. She

looked anxiously out the window as Nancy searched for street signs. "I got a call from the dean's office early this afternoon."

"Are they on your case, too?" Nancy asked.

"They left a message on my machine," George said miserably. "The dean wants to see me, Pam, Eileen, and Jamal this afternoon."

"Maybe we can work something out before then," Nancy said with a hopeful smile.

George shoved back her dark hair with both hands. "If we can't prove someone *else* is running a scam, we're going to be accused. And we have no way of proving we're innocent."

"Not now, anyway," Nancy noted, heading toward the familiar tavern and dingy office front. "Look. That must be him, standing outside the building."

Nancy pulled over and took in the short, heavyset man standing on the sidewalk, smoking a cigarette.

"Mr. Micelli?" Nancy inquired as she and George stepped out of the car.

"Uh-huh, that's me," the man answered. He shook her hand and pointed his thumb over his shoulder toward the building. "So. You wanna take a look?"

"Yes," Nancy said. "We do. I'm Nancy Drew. And this is George Fayne."

"Pleased to meet you," Mr. Micelli said as he opened the front door. "This area, I might add, is a prime business location. A lot of big companies moving in."

"Yes, I can see," Nancy said with a wan smile, following him inside. Her eyes scanned the low ceiling, dirty beige carpeting, and single metal desk. She took a few steps toward the desk, which was bare, except for a small slip of paper. Looking down, Nancy saw that it was a strip of purple paint chip colors. The darkest purple, called Aubergine, was circled. Nancy slipped the paint sample into her pocket.

"Mr. Micelli," George spoke up. "This place looks as if it's already rented. Is it?"

"Rented?" Mr. Micelli said with an innocent face. "Well—uh—let's just say that I haven't spoken with the tenants lately, and I don't know how long-term they're going to be."

"Their business doesn't look too profitable at the moment," George noted, opening a back door and peeking into a bathroom.

Mr. Micelli cleared his throat. "That's a very good observation, miss. And so you can see that it may soon be available."

"What kind of business are your tenants in?" Nancy asked. "Maybe this isn't the right location."

Mr. Micelli narrowed his dark eyebrows. "This is a fine location." He stared at Nancy and George a moment. "Okay, ladies," he said. "What's going on?"

Nancy knew Mr. Micelli was getting suspicious, and there was no reason to hide their purpose any longer. "I'm sorry, Mr. Micelli. I know you think we're interested in renting from you, but—"

"Why do you think I came all the way down here?" he snapped back.

"We think your office space is being used by criminals," George said abruptly. "They're running a scam with student loan money. *My* student loan money, in fact."

Mr. Micelli's eyes darted nervously from George to Nancy. Then he held up his hands and took a step backward. "Hey, don't look at me. I don't know anything about the guy renting this place."

"Can you tell us who it is, Mr. Micelli?" George asked.

"Look," Mr. Micelli replied, jingling the keys in his pocket. "All the arrangements were made over the phone, and the guy paid with a money order sent to my post office box. I never saw the guy, and I didn't ask him what kind of business he was in."

"The money order must have had a name on it," Nancy said. It was clear he didn't care who was renting the office space as long as he was getting his money in the mail.

Mr. Micelli's eyes turned cold as he stepped past her and opened the door, motioning for them to leave. "His name was Lewis. Jamal Lewis."

George gasped.

"Okay? Now get out and don't bother me again."

Nancy grabbed George and hurried back to the car.

"We know it's not Jamal," George said. "Someone must have used his name. Someone at Wilder."

"Maybe even someone who worked with Jamal at the student loan office," Nancy replied. "Whoever is pulling this scam had to have access to the loan office stationery."

"Right," George said, "it could have been any one of the people in that office."

Nancy looked at George. "I think we should stop by the loan office tonight—when it's, um, quiet, to see what we can find."

"Good idea," George said.

Nancy held up the paint chip she'd slipped off the office desk. "I found this in the office."

George studied it. "Aubergine. I don't know what a paint chip has to do with loan scammers."

"I don't either," Nancy said, starting the car and heading back to campus.

Nervous, worried, and determined was how Stephanie felt as she flew in the front door of Berrigan's that afternoon.

I just have to see him for five minutes, Stephanie thought to herself. She scanned the floor packed with people and merchandise for a glimpse of Jonathan. Then she hurried toward the cosmetics counters and pulled one of her co-workers aside.

"Have you seen Jonathan?"

The woman pointed. "He's taking care of something over in menswear."

Stephanie made her way toward the wood-paneled menswear department with its piles of golf sweaters.

She stopped to check her lipstick in a mirror, still feeling confused and heavy with guilt. She'd been with Jonathan the night before at the football rally, and they'd had a great time. But she couldn't shake the memory of her encounter with Mike behind the trees.

Why did I do it? Why did I have to get involved with Mike in the first place? She shook her head in confusion, hoping that just the sight of Jonathan would wipe away the still-lingering taste of Mike's kisses on her lips.

She found Jonathan deep in serious conversation on the phone near the menswear cash register. When she caught his eye, she saw his face light up. A few moments later he hung up, walked over, and gave her a quick kiss.

Stephanie felt her knees go weak. "Hi."

"What are you doing here?" Jonathan asked, slightly worried. "Don't you have a class?"

"I skipped it," Stephanie said, taking his hand and pulling him into a discreet corner near the alterations desk. She wrapped her arms around his waist and felt his crisp shirt, cool and solid under her cheek. Then she looked up at him and brushed a lock of his brown hair off his forehead. "I—I just had to see you."

Jonathan looked down and took her face between his two hands. "Steph? Is everything okay?"

The love in Jonathan's face almost made Stephanie faint. His dark eyes seemed to take her inside of him, where everything was secure and good. "Yes—yes, everything's okay now."

"Good," Jonathan whispered back. He kissed her on the forehead, on the neck, behind her ear. "I want to see you tonight, but I can't. I've got to work."

Stephanie's heart swelled. "Okay," she said as he released her. She stole one last glance into his eyes before she turned to go. But the heavy feeling in her chest was still there. The guilt still weighed her down, and she knew the only way to get rid of it was to stop fooling around with Mike.

"I swear," Stephanie whispered to herself, leaving Jonathan heading back onto the floor, "that I will be true to Jonathan. He's the only one in my life."

"I think I'll put my head under a pillow and cry now," George said gloomily as Pam opened the door to their dorm room.

"I might as well go full-time at Berrigan's and sell clothes for the rest of my life," Pam moaned, throwing her keys on her desk. "Without loan money, we can just about kiss our career plans goodbye."

Fifteen minutes earlier, George, Pam, Jamal, and Eileen had met with the dean of students in the administration building. Like Mrs. Hill, the dean had treated them as if they were suspects in a criminal investigation. Luckily, two more students had come forward to complain about the University Loan Servicing Center taking their money. But the dean still seemed to suspect that they were part of a general student fraud.

George squeezed her eyes shut, trying to block out the horrible memory of the scene in the dean's office. Wilder wasn't taking any official action against George, Pam, and Eileen, the dean had said, but they were launching an investigation.

"We'll just have to see how Wilder's grand conspiracy theory plays itself out," Pam muttered.

"Yeah," George said with a bitter laugh. "They'll figure it all out. First, we took our loan money and hid it in a secret bank account so we could buy luxury cars and new CD players. Then we all marched right into the loan office and pretended we were robbed. I've never been so mad in all my life!" George cried.

"And I've never seen Jamal so upset," Pam said quietly.

George nodded. After the meeting with the dean, she had told Jamal that the loan scammers had used his name when they rented Mr. Micelli's office space. The news had made Jamal so angry that he stormed out of the building, saying he needed a long walk to cool off. Eileen was devastated, too, and she had left to go find Emmet, who was getting ready to play in the championship game that night.

Working off steam at the Norsemen game was probably a great idea, thought George. But she and Nancy had other plans.

George rolled over on her side and spoke to Pam. "Nancy and I are going over to the student loan office tonight while everyone's at the game. We're going to try to dig up something that might throw some light on this loan scam."

Pam nodded. "I wish I could go with you, but I've got to work tonight." She checked her watch. "In fact, I'm late now."

The phone rang and George picked it up.

"George?"

"Bess!" George exclaimed, sitting back on her bed. "I've been trying to reach you."

"I just heard the bad news about you losing your loan money," Bess said. "Brian told me."

Thank you, thank you, thank you, George thought to herself. It had hurt her not to have Bess around, especially now. Quickly, George ran through the details of her loan problems and let Bess know about their plans to hunt through the student loan office that night.

"I'm coming with you," Bess said quickly.

"No way," George pleaded with her. "It's not a good time for you to get mixed up in this, Bess."

"I'm not going to let you down again," Bess said firmly. "And it may just be the right time for me to get involved, George. Trust me."

Chapter 8

"Well, that was fun. I'm glad I ran into you, Casey," Nancy said as they headed out of the elevator for their third-floor suite.

Casey smiled. "You needed some laughs with dinner?"

Nancy grinned as she nodded. "Yeah, as a matter of fact, I did."

"Come on in for a sec," Casey said, opening the door to her room. "Let's talk some more."

Nancy was happy she'd run into Casey when she'd gone to the cafeteria for an early dinner. Between Bess's problems, tension with both Jake and her dad, and George's stolen loan money, Nancy needed a little fun time with someone.

"How did you get my phone number, Mike?" Stephanie was speaking into the phone as Nancy and Casey entered. She sat stiffly on the edge of her bed, gripping the receiver with one hand and chewing a shiny red nail on the other.

Casey gave Nancy a look as they tiptoed inside.

"No, I'm sorry, but I can't," Stephanie was saying in a strained voice. Nancy noticed Stephanie's beautiful, tanned forehead was furrowed with worry. "I made a mistake, Mike. I'm involved with someone else. Okay? I can't see you again—*ever.*"

Nancy stretched out on Casey's bed and propped her head up on one elbow. Stephanie scowled and put down the phone abruptly.

"Ooh . . ." Nancy wagged a finger playfully at Stephanie. "Wait until we tell Jonathan that the guys still won't leave you alone. He's going to be *soooo* jealous."

"Hey, Nancy"—Casey nudged Nancy in the side, giving Stephanie a sly look—"give Stephanie a break. She's never said no to a guy before in her life."

Stephanie lit a cigarette and inhaled deeply, glowering at Casey. Nancy knew that Casey had said something that was true, and Stephanie couldn't deny it.

"Anyway, don't blame the guys," Casey said. "Stephanie's the one who's doing the chasing."

Stephanie's brown eyes seemed to crackle with anger. "Keep your nose out of my business, Casey," she said tightly, standing up. She rubbed the sides of her arms nervously, looking out the window while Casey and Nancy sat still in surprised silence.

"Sorry, Steph," Nancy said at last. "We didn't mean to—"

"And if you say *anything* to Jonathan about this," Stephanie snapped, turning to give them a hard stare, "I'll kill you both, I swear it."

"Stephanie!" Casey gasped. "We were just joking around."

Nancy was stunned. "Of course we would never say anything about other guys being interested in you," Nancy reassured her quickly. "We know how much Jonathan means to you. He's a great guy."

"Nancy!" She heard her roommate, Kara Verbeck, calling down the hall. "Phone!"

Reluctantly, Nancy left, wishing she had more time to talk to Stephanie. It was clear Jonathan had gotten under Stephanie's skin—the first guy Nancy had seen get close to Stephanie all year. She could tell Stephanie wasn't used to being vulnerable. Maybe she *was* in love, Nancy thought to herself. Stephanie was usually so in control. And nothing could make a person feel more *out* of control than being madly in love.

"It's your father," Kara told her when she was back in her room.

Nancy took the phone, suddenly remembering his unreturned phone messages. "Dad?" she said into the phone.

"Hi, Nan," her father said.

Nancy tightened her grip on the receiver. "I'm sorry I haven't returned your messages, Dad,"

Nancy tried to explain. "Things have been totally crazy around here."

"Pretty busy?" Carson said, and Nancy detected a weariness in his voice.

"I'm up to my neck, yeah," Nancy said, unable to think of what more to say to him.

"How's Jake?" he asked. "I liked him very much, Nan."

Nancy cleared her throat, feeling more uncomfortable and impatient by the second. She knew her father wanted to know why she'd been so angry with him and his girlfriend, Avery, during her visit. But it was clear he found the whole subject just as touchy as she did. "Jake's even busier than I am," she said finally.

"Nan . . ." Carson began carefully. "Something was bothering you last weekend. And the comments you made to Avery and Hannah the morning you left were very upsetting. But you had to leave so suddenly that we didn't have a chance to sit down to figure out what—"

"Dad," Nancy said impatiently. "I'm sorry I had to leave River Heights so suddenly. Something important came up."

"Nan," Carson replied. "We've always talked our problems through and—"

"I can't talk right now," Nancy interrupted. She knew she should discuss her feelings with him, but it was too difficult. A part of her felt guilty about blowing up at Carson, Avery, and Hannah. But another part was angry at her dad for not understanding why.

"Okay," Carson said slowly.

Nancy tensed. Why was it so difficult for her father to figure it out? It had been Nancy's first visit home from college, and her father had his girlfriend at the house the entire time *and* she'd made redecorating plans! Even Hannah, who'd been the Drews' housekeeper forever and was like a mother to Nancy, had acted differently, treating Nancy's visit like something unusual. On the surface everything had appeared to be normal—especially to Jake. But to Nancy things had been very different. She'd suddenly felt like an outsider in her own home.

"Look, Dad," Nancy finally said. "Let's talk about this another time. George is having some serious problems, and I'm supposed to be meeting with her in a just a few minutes."

"Okay, but soon," her father said firmly.

"Soon. I promise," Nancy said, hanging up the phone, grabbing her purse, and running out of the room.

Ray sat on the chair in his dorm room, strumming his guitar slowly. He picked out a few slow notes, playing with a new tune he'd thought of that afternoon. Then he stopped and burst into a fast-paced guitar riff before ending his ballad.

Ray slipped onto his bed and kept playing with the guitar on his stomach. He smiled to himself. He'd had a second jam session with Austin and Cory that afternoon, and together they had really poured it on. Austin's drumming was fluid and strong. Cory, in addition to playing the bass guitar like a madman, had a decent backup voice. Their sound was so strong that they blew through the two-hour session, barely stopping for food or drink.

Even better, some of the songs that he'd had trouble with were coming together now, with Cory and Austin's help. It was almost too good to be true.

"I'm doing it, Ginny," Ray whispered into thin air. "I'm getting it back together." Sure, he'd stick with his plan to take business courses and keep part of his brain on a practical wavelength. He was determined not to let anyone cheat him again in a business deal. But now he knew that his music wasn't over. Music was his life. Did anyone understand this better than Ginny?

Swinging his legs over the edge of his bed, Ray sat up. Putting his guitar down, he grabbed the phone and impulsively punched in Ginny's phone number as he had done a thousand times before.

Ray's heart began to beat hard as he listened to her phone ring. What would he say to her? What if someone were with her? Without realizing it, he'd begun to break out into a cold sweat. What was he doing? He and Ginny had broken up!

"Hi, this is Ginny and Liz," Ginny's quiet voice spoke from the answering machine she shared with her roommate, Liz Bader. "We can't come to the phone right now, but—"

Ray jammed the receiver back down and

closed his eyes. A hundred memories of Ginny floated through him. The soft, sweet way she used to hum his songs while she studied. The silkiness of her straight, black hair against her cheek. The time they stayed up until dawn, walking the campus and talking about music and family and dreams and love.

"It's all different now," Ray said to himself softly. "A whole new gig."

For a while Ray just sat there in silence, staring at the wall and hearing the music in his head. Then, without hesitating, he punched in Montana Smith's phone number and waited for her to answer. He'd tell Montana about the jam session. She wanted everything to go well for him, Ray thought. After all, at this point she probably cared about him more than anyone else on campus.

"Don't you think the student loan office will be closed?" Bess asked Nancy and George as they hurried across the campus quad toward the administration buiiding. The clock on the building's tower had just chimed eight o'clock, and the lights in the nearby library burned brightly. A few minutes ago the three friends had met in front of Thayer Hall for their planned visit to the student loan office.

"Jamal says the staff sometimes works late," Nancy explained, digging her hands deep into here jacket pockets. "But usually there are only a few janitors in the building between eight and eleven o'clock."

"We're hoping the door is open and the janitors don't notice us," George said.

Bess thought quickly as she walked. "Maybe I could distract them if you see something interesting."

Nancy put an arm across Bess's shoulders and gave her a hug as they hurried along. "That would be a big help, Bess."

"Thanks, Bess," George murmured. "It means a lot to me that you're here."

Bess felt warmth zip through her. "Distraction," she joked. "You know me. I'm practically majoring in distraction this year."

Actually, Bess thought, coming with George and Nancy was the best thing she'd done in weeks. When Brian had told her that George's money had been stolen, his story jerked her back to reality. She had friends who needed her. And what she needed more than anything right now was to think about them—not about herself.

Nancy squeezed Bess's hand. "I know we've all asked you a thousand times, Bess. But are you doing okay? We've been so worried."

"Yes," Bess said cautiously, as if she were really thinking about the question for the first time. She took a deep breath of a cool night air. "Yes, I think I am. In fact, I saw a counselor this afternoon. A woman Leslie recommended."

"That's great," George told her. "Really great."

"I'm not sure if it's going to work out with this counselor," Bess admitted as they started up the steps to the administration building's front door, "but I'm going to stick with it for a few sessions."

"Looks pretty quiet in there," Nancy whispered, pushing open the front door.

Once inside, the three walked cautiously into the carpeted lobby. Bess followed as Nancy and George headed down a hallway that branched to the right. Bess felt a surge of purpose that seemed to cut through the hazy depression of the past few weeks.

All three girls were quiet as they approached the office, and Bess immediately detected voices from inside.

"Yes, but your federal loans will be applied first to the tuition portion of your bill," Bess heard a woman explaining. As they entered, she could see a woman sitting at a desk across the room. A girl sat in a chair next to the desk.

"That's Marsha Sorenson," George whispered. "She was awful to us this morning."

Bess studied her. The woman looked exhausted as she explained a financial form to the student.

"Okay, Mrs. Sorenson," the student said, paper-clipping some documents together. "I've got it."

Mrs. Sorenson nodded and checked her watch. Then, as the student was gathering her things to leave, the woman quietly opened a desk drawer and slipped something out. Bess couldn't see what it was because the desk blocked her view, but she noticed Mrs. Sorenson bend down, as if she were tucking something in a purse or a bag. As she straightened up, Mrs. Sorenson saw the three girls and gave them a sharp look.

"Yes?" Mrs. Sorenson said, her eyes darting around the room. "Did you need something?"

"We're trying to track down Jamal Lewis," George said. "Is he still working?"

"He left hours ago," the woman snapped, standing up.

"I'm also looking for information on performing arts scholarships," Bess said quickly.

Mrs. Sorenson's lips pursed tightly. "As you may be aware, it is eight o'clock," she said impatiently. "And we're closed."

Bess noticed as she stalled Mrs. Sorenson, that Nancy was scanning the room for anything that might be unusual.

"When do you open in the morning?" Bess went on innocently.

Mrs. Sorenson glared at her as she switched off her computer and picked up a purse and a canvas bag that had been sitting next to her office chair. "At nine o'clock," she said between gritted teeth. "And now if you'll excuse me . . ."

"Oh, no." Bess pretended to be oblivious to Mrs. Sorenson's irritation. "I have a class then. And I just *have* to get the forms for those scholarships." Bess leaned forward intently on the counter, and as she did she was able to glimpse something in Mrs. Sorenson's open canvas bag as she marched by.

Bess was excited when she realized what was in the bag. But by this time, Mrs. Sorenson was jingling her keys and holding the office door open for them.

"I'm sorry, you'll just have to come back tomorrow," Mrs. Sorenson said grimly.

"Well, thanks anyway," Bess said as they left. George and Nancy followed as they headed down the hall, out the main door, and down the steps into the cool night. As soon as Mrs. Sorenson was out of sight, Bess grabbed George and Nancy.

"Did you see?" Bess said excitedly. "The paper Marsha Sorenson slipped out of her desk and put into her bag. It was a stack of blank Wilder University stationery!"

Chapter 9

Jake stood at the entrance to Holliston Stadium waiting impatiently for Nancy. He heard a thunderous cheer in the distance, and the Wilder University marching band started playing a triumphant song. The Norsemen must have scored, and he'd missed it. A few other latecomers raced through the main gates as Jake debated whether or not he should give up on Nancy and go inside to watch the rest of the game.

That afternoon a reporter from the *Wilder Times* sports department had unloaded two box seats on him. They were some of the best seats in the stadium, and Jake was eager to see this game. He probably should have asked his roommate, Nick, to go, but he'd wanted to see Nancy. When he'd received the last-minute tickets this afternoon, he'd tried to call Nancy, but she was out and he'd left a message with her roommate, Kara.

Jake scanned the entrance area again, but Nancy was nowhere to be seen. He saw a slender girl with long, dark hair hurrying past, followed closely by a guy with short, blond hair. "Stephanie?" Jake called out. Her tight-fitting outfit and knockout figure were unmistakable.

Stephanie looked up, and Jake saw her frown slightly when she saw him. But she stopped and, putting a seductive smile on her face, said, "Jake, where's your little Nancy?"

"That's what I was going to ask you," Jake said, ignoring her sarcasm. "I left a message with Kara for Nancy to meet me here. Have you seen her?"

"Oh, Jake," Stephanie said with mock sadness as she drummed her row of glossy red nails on the hip of her leather skirt. "Can't Nancy drag herself away from the newspaper to spend a few moments with her sexy boyfriend?"

Jake was impatient. He should have known better than to ask Stephanie for help with Nancy. He changed the subject. "Aren't you going to introduce me to your friend?" he said, nodding at the blond guy standing behind Stephanie.

Stephanie cast a nervous glance over her shoulder at the guy, "Oh, my gosh," she said, making a show of checking her watch, "Sorry, no more time for chatting. We have to run. We're meeting some people inside. See you later." Stephanie waved as she grabbed the hand of the blond guy and raced off through the entrance to the stadium.

Jake shook his head. "Yeah right," he said. What was that all about? She sure got nervous when he asked about the guy she was with. And where was that boyfriend of hers, Jonathan? Oh, who cares, Jake thought. He was in no mood for Stephanie and her games tonight.

He looked down, finally deciding Nancy never got his message. In the distance he could hear the yelling, foot-thumping crowd, but all he could think of was Nancy. Where was she?

He clenched his jaw and headed for his seat alone. He and Nancy had had so much fun at the rally the night before. The tension from the weekend at River Heights was beginning to melt. But now this.

"Oh, well," he muttered. "Something important must have come up."

"She did it," George said. "She actually took blank stationery from the office right in front of our eyes. There's no way Marsha Sorenson isn't involved in the loan scam."

Nancy cupped her hands around her coffee mug. She, George, and Bess had headed over to Java Joe's after their trip to the student loan office. It was past nine o'clock, but the café was practically deserted, since almost the entire student body was crammed into the stadium watching the game.

"Maybe we're jumping to conclusions?" Bess asked.

"No," George replied.

"Just because she put blank stationery in a bag doesn't mean she stole your money," Bess said.

"It might," Nancy said thoughtfully. "We don't really know much about Marsha."

"Exactly," George replied. "Think about it, Nan. She knows all about student loans, she knows Jamal, she's sneaking blank stationery out of the building."

Nancy leaned forward on her elbows, looking first at George, then at Bess. "Did you happen to see what was on Marsha's desk?"

"What?" George asked, surprised.

"It was a travel brochure," Nancy said. "For the Virgin Islands. It was from the Weston Getaway Travel Agency. You know, that place right off the plaza downtown."

Bess shrugged. "That doesn't prove anything."

"There was a Post-It note attached to it," Nancy went on, "that said Wednesday four P.M. I think it's worth checking out."

George narrowed her eyebrows. "She could be scamming me and Pam and Eileen so she can take off for a very long vacation in the Caribbean."

"She did seem stressed out," Nancy said. She thought about Mrs. Sorenson as she sipped her coffee. Why would a middle-aged woman with a good job at a university risk going to jail for an exotic vacation? All of Nancy's instincts told her the pieces of the puzzle weren't falling the way they should. "There was no reason for her to be so rude to us tonight in her office," she said out loud.

"She probably figured we were on to her," George said with a frown.

A thought zinged into Nancy's head. "What about Greg Pawling? Remember that guy we met who works with Jamal at the loan office? Let's talk to him about Marsha Sorenson. Maybe he knows something."

"Pam and I should be able to track him down tomorrow," George said quickly, her eyes brightening as a noisy crowd of Norsemen fans poured in through Java Joe's front entrance. "Hey, we may have missed the game, but we're not going to miss all of the action."

"Looks like we won," Bess said triumphantly, raising a victory fist. "Ya-hoo."

"Hey, Nancy!" a deep voice was calling out from among the hoots and cheers.

Nancy turned around and saw Terry Schneider approaching with a group of guys still waving Norsemen banners on little wooden sticks. She grinned and waved. "I take it we won."

"We creamed them!" Terry shouted as everyone moved in behind him, grabbing tables and chairs and waving menus. "It's crazy out there."

"Completely nuts!" Nancy yelled back, getting into the spirit. She scooted over in their booth to make room for Terry.

Someone cranked up the music on the restaurant's sound system. People began dancing. Football fans were everywhere, hooting and hollering. Terry impulsively grabbed Nancy's hands from across the table and together they did a little victory dance over the coffee cups. Nancy was giggling crazily when she heard a voice behind her.

Still laughing and singing, Nancy turned her head and saw Jake's face, which looked strangely serious in the giddy atmosphere.

"Hi!" Nancy called out, though her thoughts were suddenly focused on her hands. She looked down, embarrassed, and quickly withdrew them from Terry's grasp. "Where have you been?"

Jake sat down next to George at the end of the booth and cleared his throat. His eyes darted across the table to Terry. "Um, I've been to the game, Nancy. Didn't you get the message I left with Kara?"

"No—no, I didn't," Nancy said. "Kara must have forgotten."

"Yeah," Jake said, tapping his fingers nervously. His eyes darted in Terry's direction, and Nancy was going to explain that Terry had only just arrived at the table and that they hadn't gone to the game together.

"I had two great seats at the game," Jake called out over the commotion. "I waited for you by the stadium entrance through most of the first half."

Nancy gasped. "Oh, no. I'm really sorry. It would have been fun. But even if I'd known, I couldn't have gone, Jake. I had something I had to do."

"Breaks," Jake said, and Nancy could tell he was trying to be casual about it. Still, she didn't like the way he kept looking over at Terry, as if he expected an explanation from both of them.

Trying to shake the confusion, Nancy gave Jake a playful nudge with her foot under the table. She wasn't going to let the awkward situation make her feel bad, because she knew that everything between her and Terry was completely innocent.

Jake was the guy she loved, and he was mature enough to understand that. Wasn't he?

"Hi, Stephanie," the answering machine blared. "It's Glen."

Stephanie looked at the clock, then crawled back under the covers. Why did she have to punch that stupid button on her phone machine? The message was obviously left late last night. And she didn't want to hear it anyway. Stephanie sighed and closed her eyes trying to block out the memory of yet another guy she couldn't resist. "Just wanted to say good night, baby," the guy said. "I had a great time with you at the game. Just my good luck to stand behind you in line for those tickets, huh?"

Stephanie groaned.

"Strangers in the night, I guess, huh, baby?" the guy asked.

Stephanie sat up and got out of bed. What was

she doing? Glen. Glen the tall, blond soccer player who'd been standing next to her for only a few minutes as she got her tickets for the game. He was so funny and sweet. By the end of the first quarter, he was tickling her neck and asking how she got the little scar on her collarbone. And by halftime, she and Glen had retired to a dim area behind the refreshment stand. She never could resist the athletic type.

When she finally opened her eyes, she saw that Casey had come back from the shower. And from her expression, it was pretty clear she'd heard most of Glen's juicy phone message.

"Strangers in the night?" Casey asked, her face serious.

Stephanie hit the machine with her fist to turn it off, then crawled back under the covers.

"Glen?" Casey said loudly, whipping Stephanie's covers back halfway. "You've got to be kidding me. First Mike, now Glen?"

"Shut up, Casey," Stephanie said quietly.

"Whatever happened to that guy named Jonathan?" Casey went on. "Remember Jonathan? Nice, sweet, smart, devoted Jonathan?"

Stephanie felt tears pulling. "Stop it, Casey. It's none of your business."

"But I'm worried about you, Steph," Casey insisted, sitting down on the bed. "I'm not trying to make you feel guilty or tell you what's right or what's wrong. I'm just completely confused. Besides, I need to know. I'm the one taking your phone messages. What if I slip up and say the wrong thing to the wrong guy?"

"Gee. It must be hard for you."

"Hey," Casey said sharply. "I grew up a kid star in Hollywood, and I've seen it all, okay? And I've known lots of beautiful girls who've had love looking them right in the eye. And to these girls, it was the scariest thing in the world, so they played around. And it wasn't because they were happy and well-adjusted, Steph. They played around because they were totally mixed-up-crazy-hurt. They couldn't love because they didn't think they were lovable."

"Was that a topic on a daytime talk show?" Stephanie cracked, rolling her eyes.

"Stephanie," Casey warned.

Stephanie started to snap back but stopped herself. She lay still and silent on her bed. "I don't know what I'm doing," Stephanie finally said in a soft voice.

"Jonathan loves you," Casey said gently.

Stephanie nodded. "I know. I can't figure out why I'm goofing around with these guys. Mike doesn't mean anything to me, and neither does this Greg—I mean Glen."

"You'd better be careful," Casey warned.

"I realize that," Stephanie said. "Or I'll lose the best man and the best relationship of my life. If only I could stop. . . ."

"You are not going to believe how cool this new club is," Eileen was saying with enthusiasm.

"When you're inside," Emmet explained, heading toward the downtown area in his car, "you completely forget that you are in Weston, Illinois. It's more like Chicago."

George grinned. "Weston's okay. We have the Norsemen," she cracked.

Emmet and Eileen gave each other victory signs as George stretched her legs out sideways in the backseat. Things had been so anxiety-producing and confusing the past few days that she decided to skip her morning classes. Eileen and Emmet were meeting Emmet's brother, Jason, to get a sneak preview of the hot new club he was opening next week.

"It's in the old warehouse district," Emmet explained, slipping on his sunglasses. "A lot of these old brick buildings are being turned into restaurants and shops. It's pretty cool."

"This is great," Eileen said as Emmet led them under a black-and-silver awning that read Club Z. The three strode through a metal door into a dim, cavernous space. George could hear rock music blaring from a nearby stereo. Nails were being pounded. A distant drill whirred in the background.

"Wow," George gasped, staring as they walked under a high arch. The club was much bigger and more ambitious than she'd imagined. From where she stood she could look up and see the ceiling two stories up. The space was ringed inside with an elaborate system of stairways and multilevel metal platforms arranged so that every seat would have a view of the huge wooden dance floor below. A large bar flanked one side of the first level, where there was another space for tables and chairs. An elaborate neon sign in the shape of a hundred Z-shaped lightning bolts blazed over the dance floor.

"Jason wants the club to be a very high-energy place with lots of alternative bands and hot music," Emmet said proudly.

"Hi." A young guy with Emmet's sturdy build and sandy hair strode toward them. His face resembled Emmet's, but he wore his hair long and tied back in a ponytail. He had on a dressy sport coat and slacks.

"Hey, Jase," Emmet said warmly, grasping his brother around the shoulders in a mock tackle. "Looking good."

"Been to a meeting with my banker," Jason joked, holding out the lapels of his sport coat with a sheepish smile. "So I'm duded out." His eyes twinkled at Eileen.

Eileen laughed. "This is my friend George Fayne. George Fayne. Jason Lehman."

"Great place," George said eagerly.

"Come on and look around," Jason offered, strolling farther inside the building. "As you can see, we've got our platform seating system up now, though the design turned out to be a real hassle."

"Expensive?" Emmet asked, catching his drift.

"You bet," Jason said. "All the engineers and inspectors got together and decided we needed more elaborate reinforcements. Then, after we played around with a bunch of different sound systems, we decided on one that just shook this place up. And, of course, that cost a fortune, too."

Emmet whistled.

"I finally took in a second investor so I could cover my expenses, finish the construction, and open on time," Jason admitted.

"When is that?" Eileen asked eagerly.

"Next week," Jason said, crossing his fingers in the air. "Our kitchen and supplies will be ready tomorrow. Then we'll have an employee shake-down and a few trial runs. The band should blow everyone away, so I'm hoping that will distract from our opening night imperfections."

George shook her head. "You must be going nuts. I never realized how many details had to come together before you opened a club."

"Enough to make your head spin," Jason said good-naturedly, though George could see circles under his eyes.

A slender guy with light brown hair caught George's eye. He had been painting a section of the back wall but now was stopping to talk to someone.

"Hey," George called out, walking up to him, "Greg Pawling. Is that you?"

The guy turned and smiled. He set down his paint roller and wiped his hands on his pants. "Oh, hi, George."

"Hi," George said. She'd been hoping to run

into Greg again, since he was the guy Jamal worked with at the loan office. Even in the midst of the nightclub's exotic atmosphere, she was still focused on digging up any information she could about the scammers.

Greg wiped his forehead with the back of his wrist. His wispy hair clung to his neck with perspiration. "Whew. It's been crazy around here trying to get ready. We've been here since six."

George became serious. "I've been wanting to ask you about something. Is this a good time?"

Greg gestured for George to sit down on a nearby box. "Shoot. What's the problem?"

"Well." George took a deep breath. "I know you work at the loan office."

Greg cleared his throat. "Yes."

"It looks like my student loan money has been stolen," George said bluntly. "And—and I'm just looking for people who might be able to help me figure out how it happened."

Greg looked shocked. "That's terrible."

"I know," George said solemnly. "I got this letter from the university asking me to send my loan check to a downtown Weston business for distribution. But it turned out to be phony."

He shook his head. "And now you're out a few grand."

"Exactly," George replied. "And so are at least a half-dozen other people on campus. So, what I'm wondering is, well, have you noticed anything strange in the loan office? Anyone who's been acting weird? The loan scammer had access to university loan office stationery."

Greg pulled a rag out of his back pocket and began carefully rubbing the paint off his fingers. Finally, he said, "Well, this probably doesn't amount to anything, but there's Marsha. . . ."

"Yes?" George said, leaning forward eagerly.

A quizzical expression came over his face. "Marsha Sorenson, an assistant in the student loan office. She's been on edge lately." Greg held up his hands defensively. "Don't get me wrong. I'm not saying she had anything to do with this. I'm just thinking out loud, okay? She's just been a mess lately. Very, *very* touchy."

"Yes, I know," George said grimly.

"There's someone else, too," Greg said.

George's ears pricked up.

"Of course, this is probably unimportant," Greg said, "but I just happened to think of something about Jamal Lewis."

George drew back. "Jamal? What about Jamal?"

"It was strange," Greg went on. "It was a few weeks ago, the night of the Wilder-Brockton football game."

"So?" George urged him, gritting her teeth, despite her longing to tell him off. Jamal was definitely not involved in any scam—here or anywhere else in the universe.

Greg shrugged. "I just thought it was strange. I mean *everyone* on campus went to that football game. Brockton was our biggest obstacle to getting into the play-offs. Remember? But Jamal said he wanted to work late in the loan office."

George felt her face getting hot. "So, what are you suggesting?"

"Hey," Greg protested. "You asked me who could have written those letters and who's been acting strange. And—well—Marsha and Jamal have. And they both had opportunity."

"But Jamal doesn't have a motive," George snapped back. She stood up. "Jamal's friends were the ones who got ripped off—even his own girlfriend. It just doesn't make sense."

Greg stood up, too, looking sheepish. "Listen, I'm sorry, George. I didn't mean to make you angry or make any unfair suggestions. I was just trying to help."

George closed her eyes. "No, I'm sorry. I jumped all over you. I guess I'm a little on edge."

"Well," Greg said, picking up his paint pan and roller, "guess it's back to work." After getting paint on his roller, he made a long stroke of color down a section of wall. For a moment George just stood and stared at the color, her thoughts tumbling in her head. There was something about it that she couldn't put a finger on. Then suddenly she remembered.

"What's that beautiful purple color called, Greg?" George asked, trying to sound casual.

Greg grinned over his shoulder. "Nice, huh? It's called aubergine."

Chapter 10

Will Blackfeather stuffed his hands in his jeans pockets as he hurried toward downtown Weston. It was way past lunch, but scraps of victory banners and confetti from the big Norsemen win the night before were still scattered on every visible bench, rooftop, and lamppost.

"George would have loved that game," Will muttered, shaking his head sadly. It made him sick to see George's beautiful, laughing face so tense and angry the past few days. Her money worries were consuming her, Will knew. He also knew that he would have reacted the same way if his loans had been stolen.

He swung his arms back and forth and smiled. For the past two days, he'd been trying to think of something to make George happy.

Will's face fell momentarily as he approached

the auto body shop. Paul Cody had been riding his motorcycle when he was killed. Coming to this place and seeing the smashed bike brought fresh pain every time he returned.

But now he'd found a way around his feelings, and hoped he'd be able to help George, too. It had taken some time to put together his plan, but now everything was ready.

If he hurried, he might have the surprise ready for her before her first class of the afternoon.

"Hold the elevator!" Nancy called out as she rushed through the chrome and glass doors into the sleek Thayer Hall lobby. She was meeting George and Pam for lunch at the Student Union in a few minutes, but first she needed to pick up a textbook for her one o'clock class.

"Nancy!" Her resident adviser, Dawn Steiger, caught up to her as she reached the dorm suite door.

"Oh, hi, Dawn." Nancy turned and smiled. "What's up?"

"Have a minute?" Dawn asked, looking worried. She swung her backpack off her shoulder, went into the suite, and waved Nancy over to her room. "I need to talk to you."

Nancy checked her watch. "I've got five minutes. It's kind of how my life is this week."

"It's about Stephanie." Dawn got right to the point after she closed her door.

"Oh?" Nancy said.

Dawn sat down at her desk. "Stephanie's been a mess lately. Touchy. Crazy."

Nancy gave Dawn a knowing smile as she sat on the bed. "She's been a little touchy and crazy since the first day of the semester."

"You've got a point there." Dawn laughed, sharing the joke. "But I still need to keep tabs on her. I'm her resident adviser."

Nancy shook her head. "I'm sorry, Dawn. I think Stephanie's upset about something, too, but I just haven't thought about it much. George's loan problem has me completely distracted."

"Oh, yes, I heard about that from Eileen," Dawn said. "She's pretty worried, too. But about Stephanie—I'm going to talk to her if she isn't in better shape in the next day or two. Casey's really worried about her," Dawn said, making a note in a blue folder.

"Nice to know there's an angel watching over us sometimes," Nancy said wistfully. "I just wish there were an angel watching over George."

Dawn nodded and her blue eyes narrowed with concern. "I hear this loan scam business is a real mess."

"Eileen, Pam, and George have all lost their money," Nancy explained. "And some others, too. Now the loan office is trying to accuse them of only pretending to have been scammed. Apparently it's been done before. And when the universities reimburse the scammers, the scammers double their money."

Dawn frowned. "I've had a lot of dealings with

the loan office, and they've always been wonderful. Last year Marsha Sorenson went to bat for me when I lost some federal loan money."

Nancy perked up. "Marsha Sorenson?"

"Yeah," Dawn nodded earnestly. "She was a real sweetie. She convinced Ruth Hill to work it out so the university could grant me scholarship money instead. She made a big pitch for me."

Nancy leaned her head back against the wall and let out a breath. Had she heard the wrong name? "Marsha Sorenson?"

"Oh, she's great," Dawn went on. "She really cares about students."

"I didn't get that impression at all," Nancy contradicted. "In fact, I'm stunned."

Dawn's smile faded. "Why?"

"George and Bess and I were in her office last night, and she was quite rude," Nancy said.

"Really?" Dawn said. "Well, Marsha's going through a very nasty, expensive divorce right now. Her husband left her for another woman, and now he's fighting with Marsha over their joint property and stuff."

"Sounds awful," Nancy said.

"I guess her legal bills are practically bankrupting her," Dawn continued.

Nancy's mind suddenly went into high gear. So that could be it. Marsha could be trying to solve her financial problems by stealing loan money from students. She *did* have a motive.

"It's really sad," Dawn said.

"Yeah," Nancy said carefully, standing up. She

was suddenly very glad she'd noticed the travel brochure with the note about the four o'clock appointment this afternoon. Nancy didn't know how a fancy trip had anything to do with the high cost of divorce. But she was determined to find out.

Bess bounded up the stairs of the Hewlitt Performing Arts Center. She heard the muffled sounds of a play in rehearsal. Dancers in ponytails and leotards strolled by.

Smiling to herself, Bess walked down the second floor hallway toward the rehearsal rooms. Bulletin boards were jammed with audition results, practice schedules, and roommates-wanted notices. She breathed it all in, savoring the rich atmosphere. She hadn't realized how much she'd missed the theater until that very morning when she'd been talking with her counselor.

"And so you survived the accident, Bess," the counselor had said. "But Paul didn't."

"No," Bess had said quietly. "He didn't."

"And if you could talk to Paul right now, what would he tell you to do with your grief?"

Bess remember clearly her answer, which came as swiftly to her lips as any answer she'd ever given before. "He would tell me not to forget what I really care about. My friends. My work in the theater. Both mean so much to me. Paul would have been devastated if I dropped my friends and my acting because of what happened to him."

Right then Bess had known what she needed to do. Flying back to her dorm, she called both Brian and Casey. She needed one thing from them—their help getting her audition ready for Jeanne Glasseburg.

"Hey, hey," Brian called out from inside the rehearsal room when Bess arrived. He and Casey were sitting on a table, reading the scene Bess had planned for her audition.

"She's here," Casey sang out, looking up from the page and jumping down off the table. "Bess is gonna go for this."

Bess's heart felt full. "You bet I am." She swung her purse off her shoulder, set it down on the floor, and slipped off her jacket. "Thanks a lot for helping me."

"We're just glad you tracked us down," Brian said, patting her on the back. "We want you in Glasseburg's class with us next semester."

"Okay, let's get to work." Casey took charge, pacing the floor and talking the whole time. "Your character is a young mother and wife who has just been deserted by her husband."

"Right." Bess took a deep breath, holding the book open with her thumb as she quickly scanned the words. "I memorized it a few weeks ago. Yeah. I've got it."

Casey nodded. "Okay. Go ahead. Now, remember, it's an intense scene, and you want it to build. Don't start too high." She held her arm in the air, then lowered it. "Start the emotions down here, and let them build slowly."

Bess stood calmly in the middle of the room and relaxed, slipping into the mood of her character. As Bess worked on the scene, she felt real tears rise behind her eyes.

Then the tears began to slide down her face.

"Nice," Casey whispered.

Bess felt sobs pushing up from deep inside her. Suddenly the playwright's words had become her own. Her own pain. Her own life.

"Bess?" She heard Brian from somewhere far off. She felt a hand on her shoulder, but the hand was distant. All she could see was Paul Cody's face in front of hers. All she could feel was his memory. The sobbing began to consume her, and she felt her whole body shaking with grief. She'd cried for Paul before but never like this.

"Bess," Casey said softly, taking her hand. "It's okay. It's okay now. We're here. We don't have to do this right now. Let's take five. Or do it tomorrow."

"Okay," Bess said in a tiny voice, wiping her wet face with the back of her hand. Only a half hour into rehearsal and she was already reduced to a blubbering mess. She thought she was getting better and stronger. But now she felt shakier than ever. Would her life ever be the same again? Would she ever be normal?

"I've got time for a soda and this," George said, holding up an apple as she settled into her seat next to Nancy and Pam in the Student Union.

"You look like you're going to burst," Nancy said, biting into a burger. "What's up?"

"Listen," George said. "I've just come from that new club Emmet Lehman's brother is opening next week. You know, Club Z. It's going to be really hot. Wait till you see it."

"Maybe we could get jobs there," Pam said quietly, sipping her drink, "now that we don't have money for college."

"What's it like?" Nancy asked.

George shifted in her seat. "It's very high tech. And it's going to be very beautiful."

"So you spent all morning at a nightclub?" Nancy laughed.

George leaned forward on her elbows. "Listen," she lowered her voice. "Do you remember yesterday when you found the paint chip at the phony University Loan Servicing Center office?"

"The one that Jamal is supposedly renting?" Pam asked sarcastically. She pressed her lips into a tight, angry line.

Nancy put down her burger and gave George a serious look. "The paint chip. There's a connection?"

"There is," George went on. "Do you remember how the color aubergine was circled on the paint chip?"

Nancy nodded.

"What are you guys talking about?" Pam broke in.

Nancy's eyes were locked onto George's. "When I was in Jason Lehman's club a few minutes ago, I ran into Greg Pawling," George started to explain.

Pam nodded. "The guy who works with Jamal in the loan office. Nice guy."

George gave her a half smile. "Greg was there helping to get the club ready to open. In fact, he was painting."

Nancy's eyebrows shot up. "Aubergine. He was painting with the color aubergine?"

"You guessed it." George said.

Pam gasped. "He was painting with the same color as the chip you found in the phony office?"

"It could just be a coincidence, of course," Nancy said carefully. "I mean, anyone working with Jason on the club could have ordered the paint, right? Or could have been asked to buy the paint."

"But there's more," George went on, lowering her voice. "I told Greg all about the mess with the stolen loan money. And then I asked him if he'd noticed anything suspicious or out of the ordinary at the student loan office."

"Right," Nancy urged her on while Pam sat and stared.

George held up two fingers. "He said two things. He said Marsha Sorenson was acting really wacko lately. *And* he said that *Jamal* had acted really weird the night of the big Wilder-Brockton game. In fact, he said that Jamal—Mr. Football Fan himself—didn't go to the game because he wanted to work late at the loan office."

"He's lying!" Pam burst out. "Jamal and I

went to that game together! There's no way he would have worked that night."

George was stunned. Jamal *hadn't* worked late that night. Greg Pawling had lied to her face. But why? Was he the one who stole the money, and was he now attempting to pin the blame on Jamal?

"This is getting more interesting by the minute," Nancy said slowly.

George bit into her apple. "He even suggested that Jamal had access to the blank Wilder stationery when he worked that night."

"This is outrageous!" Pam fumed. "I'm going to track that guy down and punch him out!"

Nancy cautioned her. "Wait, Pam. That football game was a few weeks ago. Maybe he had his games or dates mixed up. It happens."

"It could still be Marsha Sorenson," George pointed out, tossing her apple core into a nearby bin. "Listen, I've got to run to my next class. It's way on the other side of campus, and we get a hard time for coming late."

Nancy grabbed her. "I dug up some more information on Marsha, and I'm going to check out that travel agency this afternoon."

George nodded. "We're still a long way from figuring this out."

The next minute George was jogging out of the Student Union and along the Mall. "Okay," she whispered to herself, pushing down her anger just to make it through the day. Focusing on a class for an hour was going to be next to impossible, she realized, since she was completely overwhelmed with worry. Would she have to drop out? Would her parents go ballistic when they heard she'd given the money away like a fool?

After hurrying around a corner, George came to an abrupt stop when she saw Will. He was standing near the entrance to the building her class was in, leaning against a shiny black sports car. His dark hair shone like satin in the sun, and his dark eyes were glowing.

"Why aren't you in class?" George asked, heading toward him. She narrowed her eyes. "Where did you get this car?"

Still smiling, Will slowly walked around to the passenger door of the car. Then, with a flourish, he opened the door and waved her in. "You—George Fayne—are taking the afternoon off."

George stared at the gleaming car. Then she focused on Will. Finally she looked at the car again and ran her fingertips along its smooth finish.

"Aren't you going to get in?" Will asked softly.

She felt a thrill go up her spine. "Whose car is this?"

Will grinned from ear to ear. "It's mine, George. All mine. Now, get in."

"I've got a class," George said absently, slipping into the front passenger seat and stretching out her legs. The seat was old, buttery leather. She was sitting low to the ground, but somehow she felt as if she were ready to fly.

"But—but how did you buy this?" George asked as Will settled into the seat next to hers.

"I sold my motorcycle," Will whispered. He took the leather-wrapped steering wheel and gripped it tightly with both hands.

George gasped. "You did what?"

Will nodded, bitting his lower lip. "The insurance company paid to have my bike fixed up like new, George. New engine. New paint job. It never looked so good, but I couldn't ever ride it again. Not after what happened to Paul."

George reached over and stroked the side of Will's face. "I understand" was all she said.

"So," Will went on, taking a deep breath. "I made a deal with the guy in the repair shop. He rebuilds old cars. I managed to trade my motorcycle for this. I had to pay a few bucks extra, but it's worth it." He turned the key in the ignition and pumped the gas pedal. Then he smiled at George. "Please don't go to your class."

"But I—I—" George stammered.

"Your loan problems are tearing you apart," Will pleaded. "I can see it in your eyes. I know it's hard for you to concentrate on classes right now. Come on. I have a plan."

George faltered. It was true she wasn't able to concentrate.

"Look," Will went on, nudging her gently, "I've made reservations for us at a place outside of town called the Swedish Baths." His eyes twinkled at her. "How does a hot tub sound to you? A massage? A Jacuzzi whirlpool?"

George finally gave in, shaking her head. "It sounds wonderful."

Will backed out of the parking spot, and George felt the exhilarating pull of the car as they sped off campus toward the highway that headed west out of town. The sky had cleared, and the whole world suddenly was big and breezy and full of hope. She closed her eyes and smiled. Will Blackfeather was the most wonderful guy she'd ever known. Even though her life at school was going to pieces, she believed she was the luckiest girl on the planet.

Chapter 11

"You got that page-one story finished, Jake?"

Jake's hands hovered over his keyboard, then plunged back down again as he finished the last words in a fury of typing. He glared at the computer screen, then turned around slowly.

Wilder Times editor-in-chief, Gail Gardeski, was draped over the top of his office partition, glaring down at him. "So. Do you?"

Jake propped his cowboy boots up on his desk and punched the Print button. "Yes, Gail, I do have the story finished," he said, grinning. "Would you edit it for me, *please?*"

"Smart aleck," Gail snorted, turning and walking away.

Jake shrugged and picked up his cardboard coffee cup, but the coffee inside was stone cold. It was just after lunch, and Jake's desk was a jumble of crumpled wrappers, half-eaten sandwiches, stacks of back copies of the newspaper, and piles of other papers.

"Hi." He heard Nancy's voice behind him. "Working hard?"

Jake spun around. He took in Nancy's face, with its perfectly straight nose and tempting lips all framed by red-gold hair. Just looking at her made his heart speed up. "Sure I'm working hard." He grinned. "At least I want Gail to think so."

Nancy sank into the chair next to his desk, fanning herself with an announcement flyer. "It's so stuffy in here," she said irritably. "How can you write when you're locked up in this hot dungeon?"

"It builds character," Jake said lightly. "Makes the rest of life a piece of cake."

Nancy rolled her eyes. She picked up a gum wrapper from his desk and began silently folding it into a tight bundle. Jake sensed her tension but wasn't sure what to say.

"What's going on, Nancy?" he finally asked.

Nancy leaned back and stared at the ceiling. "We're making progress on finding out who's behind the loan money scam. In fact, I'm going downtown this afternoon to check out something at a travel agency." She broke off as she realized Jake wasn't paying any attention.

"Look," she said, changing the subject. "I'm sorry I missed your message last night," Nancy said. "It would have been fun to go to the game with you."

Jake shrugged. "It's not that. It's just that I don't . . . What's bothering you, Nancy? Is it George?"

"Partly," Nancy said, staring intently at the folded-up gum wrapper. "I don't know. Maybe it's Bess. Or just all the pressure . . ." Nancy trailed off as she tried to smile at him. She propped her chin up and finally looked him in the eye. "Okay. I'm a mess."

Jake touched her arm. "Things haven't been the same since River Heights."

Nancy nodded. "You know, you really do have terrific powers of observation."

"Quit joking around."

"Okay," Nancy shot back, crossing her arms and staring up at the ceiling, exasperated. "I guess it's my dad."

Jake stirred in his seat. He could tell he was starting to get somewhere with Nancy, but he was suddenly very worried about where the conversation would take them.

"He's been calling me," Nancy admitted.

"Is that unusual?" Jake was fiddling with a red pen.

"No. It's just that I know he doesn't understand why I got so angry before we left," Nancy said. "And I can't explain right now."

"Yeah," Jake said. "I can tell."

Nancy sighed. "You remember what it was like that weekend. Everyone was fussing over me like I was visiting royalty."

Jake gave a slight shrug and allowed himself a brief smile. "Yeah. It was great."

"But I was in my own home. Don't you understand?"

"Uh . . ." Jake stammered, not understanding at all. "Yeah."

Nancy bit a fingernail. "Meanwhile, Avery was there every single minute. *She* was definitely not on the guest list. She was part of the household—making *redecorating* decisions. Pretty much taking over."

"Wait a minute," Jake burst out.

Nancy shot him a look. "No. You wait."

There was an awkward silence.

Finally Nancy broke it. "You don't understand," she said. "It's true that I liked Avery when she visited Wilder. But it was different in River Heights. I never had a moment alone with my dad. My home wasn't the same, Jake."

"I'm sorry, Nancy," Jake murmured, feeling the exasperation welling up. He'd been there that weekend, too, and Avery had been completely gracious. Nancy's father had found happiness with a beautiful, giving, intelligent woman. What more could Nancy want for him? Avery had done nothing to deserve the sharp comments Nancy had flung at her by the end of the weekend. It was almost as if Nancy was jealous of her. Jake wanted to call Nancy on it, but he didn't. Right now Nancy needed his support, not his criticism.

"That's okay," Nancy finally said with a tense smile. "It's hard for you to understand."

"But I *want* to understand," Jake insisted.

Nancy shrugged and turned away. "How could you? You haven't known me that long."

Jake recoiled, stung by the comment. He could feel Nancy pulling away from him, but he was determined to hang on.

Nancy's expression became sad. "Everything's changed since I left home."

Jake reached for her hand and squeezed it. "I know," Jake said lamely.

Nancy clammed up. "Uh-huh."

Jake looked down and shook his head.

"Come on," Nancy said. "I've got a story to finish. Let's talk later."

"Right," Jake muttered as she left for her desk, leaving him feeling more frustrated than ever. He wasn't giving up on Nancy, but he wondered if anything would ever be the same again.

Nancy opened the front door and walked into the pleasant front office of the Weston Getaway Travel Agency. A bell on the door jingled, and a woman on the phone behind a counter looked up.

"I'll be with you in a minute," the woman said.

Nancy smiled back.

It was four o'clock, the appointment time Marsha Sorenson had noted on her travel brochure. After an intense stint in the newsroom, followed by her two-thirty class, Nancy had hurried downtown to the agency to see if she could find out what Marsha was planning.

A second woman was on the phone behind a desk near the window, and Nancy realized with a start that the woman seated across from her was Marsha Sorenson. Mrs. Sorenson was wearing a stylish business suit, and it looked as if she'd had a complete makeover compared to her haggard appearance the night before.

Nancy was about to avert her eyes when Mrs. Sorenson suddenly looked her way and stiffened. Nancy could see that she was not happy to see her.

"I'm sorry to keep you waiting," the woman behind the counter said, hanging up the phone.

"Yes—yes," Nancy tried to think quickly. "I'm interested in a winter trip to Sydney, Australia. But I'd like to stop in Fiji and New Zealand on the way. Could you give me some fares?"

The woman started typing at her computer while Nancy glanced over her shoulder and tried to listen in on the conversation between Mrs. Sorenson and the other agent.

"Worked fifteen years in the department before being promoted to administrative assistant a year ago," Mrs. Sorenson was saying in a pleasant voice. "My duties involve supervising ten employees, many of them college students."

"Did you want a Honolulu layover, too?" the agent asked Nancy.

Nancy tried to look interested. "Yes. That would be great."

"Weekend hours are fairly regular," the agent behind the desk was explaining, "though it gets a little crazy at the end of semesters, holidays, and all vacation travel times . . ."

Nancy cocked her head with interest. From what she could tell, Marsha Sorenson wasn't planning a trip. She'd come for a job interview.

"One seat?" the agent asked, her fingers clicking crazily on the keyboard.

"Yes," Nancy said absently, trying to listen to more of the conversation. The interviewing agent was scanning a piece of paper that looked as if it might be a résumé.

So Mrs. Sorenson was looking for another job, Nancy thought. Maybe she didn't want to be working in the loan office while the authorities tried to figure out where the money went, Nancy thought.

"Thanks very much, Marsha," the agent finally said, standing and shaking her hand.

"One thousand three hundred and fifty-six dollars," Nancy's agent said, "if you fly New Pacific Airlines and make your reservation a month in advance. Would you like to do that now?"

Nancy's eyes darted toward the door, which Mrs. Sorenson was opening. "I—I'd like to think it over for a few days. Thanks."

She turned and walked briskly to the door. When she was outside, Mrs. Sorenson was standing right there, tying a scarf around her head. Nancy glanced over, and she was surprised when Mrs. Sorenson gave her a slight smile.

Nancy cleared her throat. "How did the interview go?" she asked politely. They were still standing in front of the travel agency, but Nancy didn't want to walk away. It was now or never, and she needed some answers.

"Oh"—Mrs. Sorenson waved it off—"fine, I suppose. I don't know if I'm the person they're looking for. But at least I'm out there." She turned and looked hard at Nancy. "I've seen you before in my office at Wilder, haven't I?"

"Yes," Nancy said quickly, though she was trying to keep things casual. "I was there last night looking for a friend."

"Oh!" she exclaimed. "I was a bear last night. I was so tired—so preoccupied." She gazed sadly into the distance as the cars whizzed by the plaza.

Nancy cleared her throat again, not knowing whether to leave. She could see that Mrs. Sorenson had once been a stunning woman, and she was still quite attractive with her slim figure and stylish brown hair. "Are you going back to campus now?"

Mrs. Sorenson seemed to rouse herself. The breeze fluttered her scarf, and Nancy noticed that her eyes were warm and friendly. "Yes." She shook her head and let out a nervous laugh. "I'm headed for my car. I know I must seem a little—spaced—as you students say, but I'm going through a divorce right now, and it hasn't been a picnic."

"I'm so sorry to hear you're having problems," Nancy said, walking down the plaza's brick sidewalk with her. She was beginning to feel guilty for tracking this woman down, then letting her bare her soul to her. But she had to know if Marsha could have been involved in the scam.

"Yes," Mrs. Sorenson replied wearily. "I've had to hire a lawyer, and it's been terribly expensive. Actually, I was working late last night because I need to build up my overtime. But my boss doesn't like it. Thinks I'm wearing myself out."

"So you're thinking about a weekend job," Nancy prompted her.

"Yes," she replied, hitching her purse up on her shoulder. "Weekend work would be a big help. And I've always wanted to travel." Her face fell as she spoke, and she pressed her lips together. "Still," she said carefully, "my office at the university wouldn't like it. They want our work to be full-time, a professional career, and they frown on second jobs. In fact"—Mrs. Sorenson leaned her head conspiratorially toward Nancy's—"I actually had to write a letter of recommendation for myself."

Nancy breathed in sharply. The blank stationery! "Really?"

"Oh, I know it was wrong," Mrs. Sorenson admitted. She looked over at Nancy in wonder. "I can't believe I'm telling you this. Maybe I just needed to get it off my chest."

"My lips are sealed," Nancy promised. "But how do you go about writing your own recommendation?"

"It sounds crazy," Mrs. Sorenson went on. "But I got desperate last night, thinking about this interview today and how I didn't have the recommendation I needed. So I took a few sheets of official Wilder stationery and wrote it myself. Then I signed my boss's name. If anyone finds out, I'm in deep water, of course. But then I'm already in over my head."

Nancy's head was spinning with questions. Mrs. Sorenson had another, perfectly understandable reason for taking stationery and acting strangely in the office. She may have illegally forged a letter, but she didn't seem like the sort of person who would ruthlessly steal loan money from students.

At least, Nancy didn't think so. But if Marsha Sorenson hadn't stolen the money, who had?

Ray's eyes were glued to a page of business courses in the Wilder catalog as he strolled along the Mall. It was late Wednesday afternoon, and the wide walkway with its stretches of lawn and rows of benches was fairly empty, except for a few students trickling out of the buildings.

"Contracts 301. Creating and deciphering legal contracts used in small business, copyrights, real estate transactions, partnerships, and other business enterprises. Dr. Leslie Kronsky. Graves Hall. Tu–Th 11–12."

"Yes." Ray made a fist as he stood there reading. "Something to do with actual life!"

After being fired by Pacific Records and losing his Beat Poets band to a bunch of guys in suits with complicated contracts, Ray definitely had decided to change his major from music to business. From now on, he vowed, he was going to protect himself. Running his own band wasn't just an excuse to go wild on the weekends. It was going to be a serious small business, too.

"Music Theory and Composition," Ray muttered, glancing back through the music department's course offerings. None of that made any sense to him anymore. He knew now that he could recite musical theory for the next hundred years while standing on his head. But it still wouldn't give him a recording contract or show him how to protect his music. No more nice-guy music major kicking back with his musician buddies. If his life was going to be in music, he was always going to have a foot in business, too. It was the only way to stay alive.

Ray finally looked up from the course catalog. In the distance he could see three girls heading toward him from the direction of the Student Union. Their heads were bent together and they were talking intently. Ray smiled, recognizing Montana Smith. When she spotted him, she lifted her arm and waved.

"Hi!" he called out.

Montana impulsively grabbed both girls' elbows, put her head down, and hurried forward in a playful trot, her blond curls bouncing. "Ray!"

Ray recognized her friends Nikki Bennett and Kara Verbeck, who were giggling as they ran with Montana. The wind was blowing Nikki's long hair, and Kara's green eyes sparkled as she made some laughing comment to Nikki and Montana.

"Hi," Montana panted, running up to him. Her face was very flushed and pretty. "Do you like it when women run after you like this?" she flirted.

"Oh, sure," Ray flirted back. "Every man's fantasy."

"Mmmm . . ." Montana said, smiling.

"I hear you're playing with a new band, Ray," Kara broke in.

Ray looked down at his feet. "Well, we've had a couple of sessions. Nothing official."

Montana hopped a little. "But they are very hot. As soon as you *do* become official, we're interviewing you on our show."

Nikki nudged Montana in the side. "We've been brainstorming KWDR Radio interview ideas."

" 'The Truth Behind Continental Breakfast,' " Kara said with a mock-serious face.

" 'Virtual Reality Fitness—A KWDR Radio Exposé,' " Nikki joked.

" 'Eating Too Much and Loving It,' " Montana added.

Ray laughed out loud and stuffed his course catalog into his pack.

"Actually," Montana confessed, "the show we really want to do is an interview with Jason Lehman. You know, the guy who's opening that new club next week? Club Z."

"Yeah." Ray nodded. "He's putting a truckload of money into it. Hope it works out."

"Listen." Montana linked her arm into Ray's elbow as they strolled. "We're headed over there right now to invite him to come on the show."

"Actually, we're looking for an excuse to check the place out before it opens," Kara admitted. "I mean, what else is there to do on a totally boring Wednesday afternoon?"

"Want to come, Ray?" Nikki asked.

Ray had been planning to hit the books for a few hours before dinner. But Jason Lehman was exactly the person he wanted to connect with right now. He'd heard that Jason wanted Club Z to be a showcase for new, alternative rock groups. The club might be just the opening he was looking for.

"Sure," Ray finally said. "I can't think of anything else I'd rather do right now."

Chapter 12

Nancy took a sip of her frothy cappuccino and watched Bess peel the paper wrapper off an oatmeal muffin. It was early Thursday morning, and she, Bess, and George had met for breakfast at Java Joe's. It was Nancy's first chance to tell them about her encounter with Marsha Sorenson at the travel agency the afternoon before.

"Amazing what a little blank stationery with an embossed letterhead can accomplish," George finally said after hearing Nancy's story. "It can snag you several thousand dollars of someone else's loan money."

"It can help you get a job," Bess added.

Nancy shook her head. "It's funny how something written on official-looking stationery makes people believe it must be for real."

"Tell me about it," George replied.

Bess's blue eyes were indignant. "They should keep that stuff under lock and key."

Nancy thought back to Mrs. Sorenson's plaintive look the day before. Dawn was right: the older woman *was* a sweetie, and she seemed to really care about students. "I have a feeling Mrs. Sorenson won't be forging any more letters on that stationery. She's not the type. She'll be agonizing over it forever."

"I do believe Nancy's written Mrs. Sorenson off as a suspect," George said, surprised. She gulped her coffee. "I still think there's a strong connection between her and the scam. She could have easily figured out who you were at the travel agency and tried to butter you up. I mean, how could she change from witch-woman to sweetheart-of-the-loan-office in a matter of hours? And our only other suspect is Greg Pawling. What do we have on him? A little paint chip."

Nancy shrugged and looked off, too distracted to pursue the problem at the moment. "Just following my instincts, that's all."

Bess reached across the table and touched Nancy's hand. "How are things with Jake?"

Nancy took her spoon and slowly stirred the bubbles at the top of her cappuccino. "Confusing," she said in a quiet voice.

"I don't think *he's* confused," George pointed out. "He's crazy about you."

Nancy nodded slowly, feeling the ache in her heart grow. "Yes, I know. It's just that . . ."

"What?" Bess prompted her.

"It's just that it was very strange having him home with me in River Heights," Nancy began. "It made me realize how new he is in my life. And—and how we don't really know each other that well."

"How could you?" Bess said softly. "You only met a couple months ago."

"Home was so different," Nancy went on, trying to sort through her thoughts. "Dad was with Avery. I was there with Jake, instead of Ned. To me everything was radically changed. But Jake didn't know the difference, because it was all new to him. It was totally strange."

George gave her a sympathetic look. "Things change."

"I know," Nancy said, sipping her coffee. "I just wish it weren't so hard."

"Sounds to me like you miss Ned," George said.

Nancy squirmed. "Oh, I do sometimes." Then she smiled. "Actually I *think* about Ned every time I run into Terry Schneider."

George laughed. "Terry does look like Ned. When I see him, I think it's Ned coming back to spy on you and Jake."

"Oh, stop it," Nancy said wearily.

"Ned would never do that, anyway," Bess said, staring at her cast. "He's too kind."

Nancy felt a tug in her heart.

"Ned helped me so much when he came by to see me back in River Heights," Bess said.

Nancy nodded. "That's Ned. You can say anything, and he understands. Maybe it's because he's Ned. Or maybe it's just because we've known him for so long. Sometimes I miss it."

"I poured my heart out to him," Bess admitted. "He seemed to want to know what kind of person Paul was and why I loved him. I felt a lot better after we talked."

Nancy smiled. "And he helped you see that your parents' idea about seeing a counselor wasn't so bizarre."

"Ned's the best," George said. "I miss him, too."

"And, to top things off," Bess continued, "he called me yesterday to find out how I was doing. So I told him about the counselor Leslie had recommended and how well she's working out."

Nancy stiffened. Ned called Bess yesterday?

"How cool of him," George said, "to call and find out how you were."

Nancy opened her mouth to speak, but a moment later closed it. Ned wasn't in touch with her, but he was in touch with Bess. How strange that seemed. It wasn't that she was jealous—really. Ned was the kind of guy to stay loyal to an old friend like Bess, especially after she'd gone through a devastating accident that took the life of her boyfriend.

Nancy wanted to know every detail about their conversation. What did he say? How was he? She was suddenly envious of Bess for having a closeness with Ned that she no longer had.

"Nancy!" She heard her roommate's voice behind her. She turned and saw Kara with Nikki weaving their way through the empty tables.

Nancy waved and made room around the table. "Where were you last night?" Nancy asked Kara. "I must have been asleep when you got back."

"At Club Z." Kara gushed. "It was awesome! Nikki and I went there yesterday afternoon with Montana and Ray Johansson to check it out and see if Jason Lehman would agree to a KWDR interview."

"And we ended up staying until midnight, helping with the painting and unloading and all kinds of stuff," Nikki said. She sipped her coffee, waving one hand eagerly. "The place is unbelievable. They must have had a very hot designer put the look together—"

"Because you feel like you're in another world when you're there," Kara added.

"An *intriguing* world," Nikki said with a dreamy look.

Bess put her elbows on the table and leaned forward eagerly. "I can't wait."

"Well, Jason has spent a fortune on this place," Kara explained. "In fact, he actually ran out of money at one point. The bank wouldn't lend him any more, and for a while he didn't know if he'd be able to open."

Nancy looked at her. "So what happened?"

"Greg Pawling stepped in," Kara said. "Do you know him?"

Nancy and George exchanged looks. "Yes, we do," Nancy replied slowly.

"Well," Kara went on, "in exchange for becoming an investor, Greg agreed to pay off Jason's bills and finish the renovations."

"Isn't that the coolest thing?" Nikki enthused. "I love that Greg Pawling! We helped him paint all night."

Nancy's head was swimming. She and George and Bess just sat in stunned silence as Kara and Nikki chatted happily. Greg Pawling: His name kept coming up. How would a grad student who had to work part-time in a loan office have the bucks to invest in a nightclub? Then there was the aubergine paint chip. And Greg worked in the loan office, with easy access to its stationery.

Nancy was sure now that Greg Pawling was involved in the loan scam. But they still had a long way to go to actually prove he stole the money.

Stephanie slung her shampoo bag over her shoulder and hurried back down the hall from the shower to her room. Though she'd set her alarm for seven-thirty, she didn't wake up until eight-thirty. Now it looked as if her nine o'clock class was doomed, unless she could run all the way across campus in ten minutes. No way.

Getting angrier by the minute, Stephanie wondered why Casey hadn't woken her. Did Casey have a particular need to see that she missed class?

"Hi, Stephanie."

Stephanie cringed as she saw Dawn sticking

her head out her dorm room door, waving her in. "Can I talk with you for a minute?"

Stephanie slowed and whistled under her breath. First her friends criticized her. Then Casey acted like a mother hen clucking at her. Now the RA wanted to see her. She needed a cigarette—bad.

"It won't take a minute," Dawn pleaded.

Stephanie checked her watch. "Good. Then I can blame you for making me miss my class."

"Come on in," Dawn said with a patient expression.

Stephanie padded into the room and sat stiffly on the edge of Dawn's narrow bed. Dawn sat on a chair at her desk and thoughtfully studied Stephanie. "Some of us are worried about you," she said bluntly.

"And why is that?" Stephanie asked sarcastically. The face she made didn't really fit the way she was feeling, which was angry and embarrassed. But acting was a way of life for her. It had been since she was a little girl getting her way with her dad. Besides, she knew people were talking about poor-Jonathan-if-he-only-knew. She wasn't exactly surprised that Dawn wanted to lecture her on the subject.

"We're worried because you seem upset about something," Dawn said simply.

"Well, it's nobody's business," Stephanie snapped, crossing her legs impatiently and staring out the window. What did Dawn know? She was totally screwed up herself. In fact, she had practically flipped out when she'd broken up with her boyfriend at the beginning of the year.

"It's Casey's business," Dawn came back. "She's your roommate, and she says you've been very touchy. I realize this may seem like prying . . ."

"It does."

"But we know you're seriously involved with Jonathan Bauer," Dawn continued. "And that can be a lot of pressure."

"Oh, give me a break," Stephanie drawled.

"What I mean is," Dawn said, "he's an older guy who lives off campus, away from all the activities and distractions we have here at Wilder. And—well, frankly, it can get kind of confusing sometimes. I know it's absolutely, totally your business who you spend time with, but if you need to talk, please let me know. And go easy on Casey."

"Will that be all?" Stephanie said tartly, standing up.

Dawn stared at her. "Yes, I guess it is."

"Well, then, it's time for me to speak," Stephanie huffed.

"Oh, Stephanie—"

"I'm not in the mood for your moralizing. You've made me miss my class. And, by the way, Dawn, my life is going precisely the way I want it right now," she lied, before flouncing out of the room and slamming the door behind her.

Nancy, Bess, and George were racing across the campus lawn, their feet and ankles wet with morning dew. They were headed for the Student Union Building, where they knew they'd be able to find a student directory fast. Right now their objective was clear: to find out where Greg Pawling lived and dig up the evidence they needed to prove he had stolen the loan money.

"I know he won't be at home," George panted. "Montana said he was supposed to be at Club Z at dawn this morning. They need to finish painting in time for the carpet layers this afternoon."

"Good," Nancy said, "because the longer we wait, the more chance he has to spend that money."

"If he hasn't already," Bess said grimly.

They stepped quickly onto the footpath that skirted the library. *"If* he's guilty," Nancy thought out loud. "But in my mind everything began to fall in place when we found out about Greg investing in that club. That had to be big money."

"It has to be him," George agreed as they neared the Student Union and yanked open the door. "How else would he get that kind of money?"

Nancy rushed to the phone booth, grabbed the student directory, and found the address for Greg H. Pawling. "Okay. Write this down someone. Twenty-three forty-five Alder Avenue, Apartment A."

"Got it," George said quickly.

"It's just a few blocks," Nancy reasoned. "We can walk there."

The three friends headed off campus, down a shady block, lined with older, run-down homes most of which had been turned into apartments for students.

"It's got to be this next building," Nancy pointed. "This one is twenty-three forty-three." She slowed next to the hedge separating the two buildings, and checked to see if anyone was around. Fortunately, the narrow driveway was empty and the street was deadly quiet.

"What should we do now?" Bess whispered, standing behind Nancy.

"Let's go around the back," George suggested.

"Okay, but let's knock on his door first," Nancy suggested. "He probably won't be there, but if he is, we'll just make up an excuse. . . . We'll say we wanted to know if he needs any help finishing the club. If he's gone, we'll try to find a way in."

"Okay," George and Bess agreed. They walked cautiously to the front porch of the older, two-story building. Greg's apartment was on the first floor.

Nancy knocked on the front door.

"It sounds pretty quiet," Bess said.

"I can't see anyone," George whispered, squinting in through the front window.

"Let's walk around the back," Nancy said, after trying the front doorknob. They hurried down the steps and along the side of the building. "From the look of the windows, he rents this half of the first floor. Let's see if there's a back door."

Nancy, Bess, and George continued along the side of the building until they reached the backyard. A sagging porch extended out from the back of the apartment house. Nancy quickly slipped up the steps and tried the door. "It's locked, too."

"Here." George was waving her over. Just to the right of the narrow porch, almost at ground level, was a basement window. George wiggled the handle and managed to pull it open.

Nancy, Bess, and George climbed down through the window to the space inside. It was pitch-black, but in a few seconds their eyes adjusted.

Nancy's eyes darted around the dark basement until she saw a staircase to the first floor.

The three girls made their way up the stairs. At the top Nancy tried the door handle. It turned. She pushed the door open and found herself looking into a messy kitchen.

"Come on," Nancy whispered.

As she slipped through the doorway, her gaze searched the countertops, then the view of the living room beyond. She moved forward, taking in the high ceilings, smudgy windows, and tall bookcases, stuffed with textbooks and paperbacks. A cluttered rolltop desk was set against the wall where a computer and printer were also housed. In the center of the room a beat-up couch faced a TV perched on an overturned crate.

George darted toward the desk and started

searching systematically through the stacks of statistical printouts and economics papers piled next to the keyboard. Meanwhile, Nancy began sliding open the lower drawers of the desk.

"Stand by the window and watch to see if anyone comes," George told Bess. "I think we're okay, but we don't want to be surprised."

"Since what we're doing is totally illegal," Bess muttered, positioning herself next to the window and peering out sideways.

"George—is there anything on the top of the desk?" Nancy asked as she rapidly flipped through a stack of files in the top drawer. "Anything to do with the loan office or ULSC. Receipts. Checks."

"So far, nothing," George replied.

"This place smells like old bacon fat," Bess complained, wiping her forehead with the back of her wrist. "And Greg Pawling definitely doesn't have the kind of money it takes to invest in a nightclub. The guy is slumming it big time."

Nancy nodded in agreement as she looked through the last drawer of the rolltop desk. Then she sat back on her heels and let out a sigh when she saw it. "The stationery."

George ducked down next to her and Bess hurried over. Inside the drawer was a crisp stack of stationery that read Wilder University Student Loan Office. As Nancy dug deeper into the drawer, she found a slim manila folder in the back. She held her breath as she opened it and realized she'd found what she'd been looking for.

"The letter," George said, looking down at a paper Nancy had taken out of the folder, "that was sent to me and Eileen and Pam."

Nancy felt a rush of excitement. Sure enough, it was the letter recommending the University Loan Servicing Center to students and giving the Battery Street address. The file folder was full of copies of the letter.

"What a slimebag," Bess murmured.

After taking one copy of the letter, Nancy slowly closed the file folder, then slipped it back in the drawer. She looked around the room. "Bess," Nancy said, "check that coffee table. It's covered with papers. There might be something else we can use. Then we'll get out of here."

As Bess searched through the papers on the table, George made sure the desk seemed to be untouched.

"Here's a receipt," Bess said, waving a slip of paper in the air. "Does Acme Commercial Rentals mean anything?"

"Let me see that!" George practically shouted, leaping across the room and grabbing the slip of paper. She scanned the receipt frantically, then pressed it to her lips. "It's from Micelli."

Nancy rushed over and looked at it, too. "Victor Micelli," she echoed. "The receipt for the phony office."

"We've nailed him," George said softly.

Nancy looked toward the window. "Come on, you guys. I think it's time we confront Greg."

Chapter 13

Planning on starting your own corporation?"

Ray was sipping a double espresso, staring at the business section of the Wilder course catalog for the fifth time that day. For a split second he thought he was dreaming, since the voice was so very far away and so charged with memories.

"Ray?" the voice spoke again.

He turned around, half expecting to see Montana. Then he felt something inside his chest leap up before it fell back again. He grinned and slid out the chair next to his. "Hi, Ginny."

"Business courses?" Ginny said in wonder as she sat down. She made a square with her fingers and looked at him through the frame, joking, "What is wrong with this picture?"

Ray laughed. "Why not?"

Ginny laughed, too. Her dark eyes were shining, her black hair hung loose, and her delicate face was the color of a faintly pink blossom. She was wearing a leotard top and jeans, which showed off her slender figure. Her familiar green backpack, loaded down with biology texts and lab books, was slung over her shoulder.

Ginny dumped her pack on the table. "I can't see you hanging out with all those linear minds, Ray. I'm sorry."

"I know. I'll bet my professors require me to buy penny loafers and a blue blazer before the first day of class," Ray replied. "That's okay, I'll just write a protest song about it."

He pointed at the catalog. "You gave me some good advice about staying in school. I guess I need to learn a little more about business before I venture out into the real-world music scene again."

Ginny smiled silently and shook her head. Ray shoved his espresso toward her, and she took a sip. "I really am happy you're doing this, you know," Ginny said.

"Yeah," Ray said. "I know." He took in her calm expression. Ginny had written the lyrics to some of his songs for the Beat Poets and, for a while, even thought of giving up her dreams of becoming a doctor to pursue a career in the music business with him.

"And I take it you're not letting Pacific Records keep you from making music." Ginny grinned.

"Actually, it looks like I've found a new

band," Ray explained, suddenly wanting to tell her everything. He explained about Austin and Cory.

Ginny looked impressed. "So, you're going to learn more about business to protect yourself, but you're still moving ahead with the music. That's so great, Ray." She rested her elbow on the table and cradled the side of her face in her hand. "Pretty soon you'll be the talk of the campus again."

"Really?"

"Yes, really."

"Gives me shivers just thinking about it," Ray teased back.

Ginny's face began to look a little sad.

"So," Ray said, changing the subject by brushing Ginny's chin with his knuckle, "how's your life?"

Ginny stretched out her arms and sank her forehead down to the tabletop. "Work. Stress. Volunteer work at Weston General. Classes."

"When you're a doctor I'll have to hire you to attend to me," Ray teased.

"That I'll gladly do," Ginny agreed, picking her head up. "But it's going to be a few years." She smiled. "Years of no sleep."

"But you love it," Ray acknowledged.

Ginny nodded. "I love my volunteer work in the pediatric wing right now." She shook a finger at Ray. "So, it isn't just my parents' idea about me becoming a doctor."

Ray nodded, not knowing what to say next. He

missed Ginny so much sometimes his heart ached. There was something very steadying about her. Just sitting next to her like this made him feel solid and secure again.

"In the meantime," Ginny said gently, "I'm having fun with friends. You know—football games, movies, the usual."

"Good," Ray said, grateful that she hadn't mentioned Frank Chung.

"Yeah."

"Well . . ." Ray started.

"Well, it was great to see you, Ray," Ginny said softly, and Ray knew that she meant it when she touched the side of his arm as she stood up.

"See you around." Ray said quietly.

"I want to stay in touch," Ginny said seriously, peering into his eyes as she hefted her pack onto her shoulder.

Ray smiled and nodded, then stared down into his coffee cup, not wanting to show the emotion that took him by surprise.

A few minutes later Nancy, Bess, and George were hurrying toward the entrance to Club Z. Pam and Eileen were already in front, along with Jamal and Emmet.

"Good," Nancy said. "Pam and Jamal are here."

"Eileen and Emmet, too," George added. "This is working out better than I expected."

Nancy nodded, shoving a lock of stray hair off her forehead and slowing. After discovering the incriminating evidence in Greg's apartment, Nancy, Bess, and George had rushed to a phone booth. Luckily, they were able to reach both Jamal and Pam before they'd left for class. The trap was set. Nancy and George would meet Pam and Jamal in front of Club Z, where Greg Pawling was finishing up painting.

The plan was to confront Greg with the evidence they'd found and hope that he'd confess—first to them, then to the university and the police.

If Greg tried to run, they'd hold him until they called the police.

"I just hope I don't kill Pawling with my bare hands," Jamal said, clenching his jaw.

"I hope you don't either." Pam grabbed him. "Cool down. If we get him mad, I doubt if we'll be able to get him to confess anything at all."

"Yeah, but I work with this guy," Jamal said angrily. "He's not only a liar and a thief, but he was actually willing to let me take the rap for his crummy scheme."

"Come on," Nancy said. "Let's go in and get this done."

"I've already called my brother," Emmet said soberly, "to let him know what's coming down. Pawling's definitely in there. Jason confirmed it."

When the group walked into the club, Nancy spotted Greg across the room, perched on scaffolding, finishing off another aubergine purple wall.

Jason Lehman was standing in a doorway,

across the jumble of packing crates, ladders, and paint canvases. He gave the group a brief, sober nod.

Greg turned and saw Nancy and the others approaching. His mouth spread into a grin as he climbed down from the scaffolding.

"Greg?" Jamal called out. "We want to talk with you for a few minutes."

"Sure," Greg said, hopping down from his perch. He took his painting hat off, and his light brown hair clung awkwardly to his small head. "What's up, guys? Some kind of trouble?"

"Yes, Greg," Nancy said, walking toward him, "there has been some trouble."

"We've been to your apartment, Greg," George put in.

"What?" Greg stared from Nancy to George and began to look concerned. He thrust his hands in his pockets. "What's this all about? You went to my apartment when I wasn't there?"

"Greg," George said evenly, stopping a few feet in front of him while the others gathered around her. "We know everything about your loan scam. And we're here to tell you to turn yourself in. Now."

Greg's face began to tighten. "What are you talking about?" he said angrily.

"In your apartment we found the blank university loan office stationery and a copy of the phony letter you sent to all of us, Greg." George pulled out the copy of the letter and waved it at him. "Come on. Where's our loan money?"

"The letter?" Greg said. "You broke into my apartment?" His expression turned indignant, then nervous. "Someone sent me that letter, too!" Greg blurted out. "Just like you said yesterday morning, George. Found it in the mail when I got back last night. Someone's trying to get my money, too. It's terrible!"

"You're lying, Pawling," Jamal said angrily. "You told George that I'd been acting strangely and working late in the office. You gave your sleazy rental agent my name. You were trying to pin this on me, you creep!"

Emmet had to grab Jamal's upper arm to restrain him, and Greg began to back up, holding his hands up. "W-wait a minute, guys."

"We found the receipt that Victor Micelli gave you for the rental of the office," Nancy explained. "And more copies of the phony letter are still in your apartment. You did it, Greg. You wrote the letters, set up the office, and stole the money. Then you tried to pin it on Jamal—and Marsha Sorenson, too."

Greg let out a nervous laugh. "Ha. That's absolutely crazy. Micelli, huh? Sure I'm renting from him, but it's not that office space you're talking about. It's—it's something else. Hey—I'm a grad student getting an advanced degree in econ. I don't have to take this from you."

"You're lame, man," Jamal called out. "Lame."

"Come on, Greg," Nancy tried to reason with

him. "Where did you get thousands of dollars to invest in a nightclub?"

Nancy watched as Greg's glance darted toward a side door. Every muscle in his body was tense, and his face was flushed and wet with perspiration.

"By the way," Nancy said, "we're calling the police about what we know, Greg. It'll take them only a few minutes to get here. I'm sure after we show them what we have, they'll have some questions of their own for you."

There was a slow change in Greg's face, as if he finally realized he couldn't lie anymore. He sat down on an overturned bucket and stared down at his paint-spattered shoes. There was a long and painful silence.

"Okay," Greg finally spoke, wiping his forehead with a rag and looking off to the side. "I just want you to know that everything would have worked out if you hadn't screwed things up. Everyone of you would have been reimbursed by the university. I've checked it all out. . . ." His voice trailed off. "Oh, what do you care?"

"Oh, man," Jason muttered, leaning against the doorjamb and gazing out over his nearly finished club. "You're too much."

"What happened, Greg?" Nancy asked.

Greg cleared his throat. "I read this article about loan frauds. The government doesn't have the money to track down everyone who plays around with the system. But the universities have the bucks to pay back the students who've been taken."

"Oh, yeah, right," Eileen interrupted, sarcastic. "The dean of students couldn't wait to give us our money back."

"Do you know they were ready to accuse *us* of fraud?" Pam cried out.

Ignoring them, Greg continued, "So when I found out that Jason needed an investor to get this club opened, I figured it was a great opportunity."

"Oh, man," George muttered.

"Hey," Greg suddenly snapped. "I'll have forty thousand dollars in loans to pay off once I graduate. How am I going to do that? I got desperate, and I worked out a plan. It's as simple as that. Whereas *you*"—his face suddenly turned nasty as he pointed angrily at George—"can take your innocent, fresh face right up to the dean and get a refund in five seconds."

"You jerk," George snapped back.

"So, yeah, I rented the office in town as a front," Greg went on. "Then I stole the stationery and used my laser printer to print the letters to a few people. Just enough to get the money I needed and not create a major, attention-getting scandal."

Nancy narrowed her eyes. "Why did you pick George, Eileen, and Pam?"

Greg shrugged and rubbed his eyes tiredly. "Because I knew they had loans. You were all talking about your loans one day when you came into the loan office to pick up Jamal." He let out a nasty laugh. "I picked two other guys, too. Real know-nothing morons who used to come into the loan office and jerk me around, claiming I didn't know what I was talking about and wanting to see Mrs. Hill. *That* was sweet. Very sweet."

Nancy shuddered. Greg's phony, good-guy act had disappeared.

"Was it sweet when you decided to use my name on your office rental agreement?" Jamal demanded, glaring at him.

Greg's expression grew cold. "Hey, Lewis. The whole idea here is to not get caught. Get it? Why would I use my own name? If I used *your* name and involved your friends, then they'd go looking for you, not me. What do you think I am? Some kind of idiot?"

"Yes," Jamal said simply. "Yes, I do."

Nancy glanced over at Jason, who was speaking to the police on a portable phone. Nancy felt relieved. It was time to get the police involved and see if any of her friends' money could be retrieved.

Bess walked up the front steps of the Kappa house and stopped to catch her breath. It was now early evening and it had been quite a day. After the police got to Club Z, they took Greg in for questioning and said they were going to check his bank account to see if the stolen loan money was still there. But for now, at least, Greg Pawling was in jail, awaiting a court hearing.

So much had happened in the last few hours—searching through Greg Pawling's apartment, then running to Club Z to confront him. After that she'd caught a late afternoon class, followed by another therapy session.

She rolled her eyes as she opened the front door of the Kappa house. "Life is never dull, at least," she muttered to herself, breathing in the smell of muffins baking. She grabbed the stair railing and headed up the carpeted stairs to Holly Thornton's room. She realized that the awkwardness of being a pitied victim was beginning to subside. The talks with her counselor were helping. Her friends and family were important to her as she pulled herself through this crisis, but now she knew she needed a professional's help as well. Someone objective.

"Hi," Bess said, peeking into Holly's room.

Holly was sitting at her desk, her brown eyes glued to her computer screen. Clicking her mouse with one hand, she silently waved Bess in. A flurry of typing followed, then the efficient whirring sound of her computer.

Bess stretched out on Holly's bed and propped up her tired arm, grateful for a chance to relax. Finally Holly turned around. "Hi," she said, rubbing her eyes. "It's a beautiful day, and I've spent practically all afternoon staring into a tube."

Bess raised her eyebrows. "The question is why?"

Holly's brown eyes gleamed as she leaned back

in her chair and stretched her arms straight back over her head. "Because it's a gas, that's why."

"Looking into a computer is a gas?" Bess laughed. "Right."

Holly shook her head good-naturedly and tapped a few keys. "Come over here, pal. Let me show you something."

"Uh-oh."

"Now," Holly said firmly. Bess got up and sat down next to her at the computer. "Here we go. I'm clicking into my Internet server software right now. It'll help me connect to stuff I'm interested in. Okay, so here's the Usenet Newsgroups."

Bess watched, baffled. "Okay, okay. What are newsgroups?"

Holly laughed. "They're discussion groups. You can find a newsgroup for just about anything you want. Okay. You're into the theater. Let's scroll for the theater arts newsgroup."

Bess grabbed a chair and wiggled forward. "You're kidding."

"Nope," Holly muttered, taking her mouse and dragging the menu down. What topic in theater arts are you interested in?"

"Um," Bess tried to think. "How about Broadway plays?"

"Mmmm." Holly scooted the mouse down, revealing a number of topics Internet users had logged on with. "Yeah. Here's a Broadway theater group."

Bess covered her mouth in awe as she read a

heated argument going on between two people about a current New York production.

"You can join in if you want," Holly explained. "And if you want someone to respond, you use your Internet address. See? That's my address."

"This is incredible!" Bess exclaimed.

"Yeah, I can sit here and have access to any library in the world, or basically anyone's computer, as long as they're on the Internet," Holly explained. Her mouth curved into a smile. "Currently my favorite anonymous computer out there is called BSJRwil.edu."

"What's that?"

Holly grinned. "Some guy right here at Wilder. We've been sending E-mail back and forth for a couple of weeks now. It all started when I logged into a group about graphic design."

Bess rolled her eyes. Holly was an art major, and sometimes her ideas about color and form and balance went way over Bess's head.

"I got into a big argument with this guy for three days about—well, about this design concept that's a little hard to explain. But you see, I found someone who understood. And that was great," Holly added.

"Great," Bess said, shaking her head.

"I think I might want to get to know him," Holly said seriously. Then she smiled. "But first there are three other guys I'm checking out. He'll have to wait until I'm done with my research."

Chapter 14

Stephanie followed the maître d' across the deep rose carpet. Candles illuminated each table in the restaurant. At the end of the room, a fire crackled in a river-rock hearth.

"Miss?" A waiter was holding out her chair.

"Thank you," Stephanie whispered, sitting down. The waiter placed a thick linen napkin in her lap and handed her a menu.

"Is this table okay?" Jonathan asked, smiling as he settled in with his own menu. He wore a starched white shirt, tie, and dark suit that set off his wavy, chestnut hair. It was Saturday night, and he'd asked Stephanie to pick any restaurant in town for a special date.

Stephanie looked out the window to the deck and lovely fall garden beyond, beautiful in the fading light. "I love it, Jonathan. It's perfect."

"You're perfect," Jonathan said softly, reaching out and taking her hand.

Stephanie felt her emotions welling up, and she had to stare down into the lap of her blue silk dress. Jonathan was probably the only person on the face of the planet who thought she was perfect. She wasn't, of course, and she definitely didn't deserve the love of this wonderful man sitting in front of her. With all her heart, she wished she could tell him that, but it wasn't possible for her to admit it—at least right now.

"Thank you," Stephanie said instead. She reached across the table and placed her palm on his cheek. For a while neither of them said anything. They just smiled at each other.

"You don't look hungry at all," Jonathan teased gently.

"I'm too happy to be hungry," Stephanie murmured back, gazing into his eyes and leaning back. It was a relief to be with Jonathan at such an out-of-the-way spot, which was why she suggested the restaurant. She knew she was safe from any unexpected run-ins with Wilder guys she didn't want Jonathan to get to know. It was the perfect place to get her mind focused on their relationship and to turn over a new leaf.

"Things okay with your classes?" Jonathan asked her.

Stephanie nodded. "The usual. Too many papers to write. But work was great. Two hundred and sixty dollars in sales."

Jonathan's jaw dropped. "That's terrific. Just

today? What are you telling these women to make them buy so much?"

"I tell them that they're beautiful," Stephanie said simply. "And even if they don't quite believe me, I think I give them a little hope, so they buy."

Jonathan sipped his water and nodded. "You have a knack for sales, and if you can sell, every business in the country will want you when you're out of college."

Stephanie shrugged. "I can't believe it, but I like to sell. Maybe I like to persuade people. I don't know. I just get a kick out of it."

Jonathan shook his head a little, as if he was slightly overwhelmed. It made Stephanie feel good about herself, the way Jonathan always made her feel. Then he took her hand and looked tenderly at the silver friendship ring he'd given her. She stared at his fingers, long and capable looking, and it was as if the circle of candlelight at their table was their whole world.

Every other guy she'd ever dated or flirted with simply faded into history. Jonathan was the only guy she could ever want. The only one she trusted. The only one she'd ever loved.

Slowly, Stephanie withdrew her hand and reached down for her bag. She dug out the small silver package the store had wrapped for her that afternoon. Then she handed it to him.

"What's this?" Jonathan said quietly.

"It's a gift."

He took off the ribbon and opened the small

box. Stephanie held her breath as she watched his reaction. Lying on the square of pure white cotton was a silver friendship ring.

"It's—it's just like the one I gave you, Steph," Jonathan said slowly. "The same design—two hands clasped together."

"I know," she replied, suddenly feeling shy. "I—I thought you'd like to have one, too."

Jonathan's eyes were shining. He gave an embarrassed laugh. "I guess this means you do love me after all."

"What!" Stephanie exclaimed. "Of course I love you, Jonathan. Haven't I ever told you?"

"Uh—no, Stephanie," Jonathan said. "Actually you have never said that to me. When I first told you I loved you a few days ago, well—you never responded, Steph."

Shocked and filled with tenderness, Stephanie took Jonathan's hands. "But I do. I do love you, Jonathan. You are the most wonderful man I've ever known, and the best thing to happen to me—ever."

Stephanie had surprised herself. It had been so easy to say. She didn't have to act or pretend or flirt. All she had to do was tell the truth. And it was true. Jonathan was the man she loved with all of her heart. Forever.

Well, she hoped forever.

Jamal was an excellent dancer. Grabbing both of Pam's hands, he moved her to the right, then the left, then spun her completely around, her arms high in the air. She felt dizzy, happy, and blissfully relieved all at once.

Meanwhile, everyone else at the Underground was moving like bits of colored light in the darkness. The Saturday night feel of release and freedom seemed to overcome everyone at once. But as the music slowed, all Pam wanted to do was press her cheek against Jamal's chest and take in the warmth of his shirt.

The police had checked Greg's bank account. Except for a few hundred dollars, all of the stolen loan money was still there. Luckily, Greg hadn't given any to Jason for the club yet. The police needed to keep the money as evidence for a while, but the district attorney's office had called the dean of students and guaranteed that the student victims would all have their money returned.

Within an hour Pam had rushed over to the bursar's office to see if they'd heard from the dean. They had and assured her that her tuition and dorm bills would be marked as paid until they had the actual cash back from the police.

As the dancing couples slipped by, Pam spotted George and Will dancing cheek-to-cheek in the corner, barely swaying, as if they were unaware of the crowd. Pam smiled to herself. George had been stomping around like an angry bear all week. It was good to see her so happy and content now.

The music speeded up, and Jamal released her. Then he stooped down playfully and pretended to photograph her while she danced alone.

"Stop!" Pam laughed.

"Yeah, okay," Jamal called out, goofing. "Big smile. Just like that, gorgeous."

Pam made a pouty face. She was in too good a mood to mind Jamal's joking. The day before she'd heard from the Natural Shades Company, a cosmetics firm launching a new line of cosmetics made especially for young African American women. A few weeks earlier company representatives had visited Wilder University on a search for a new model to represent the line. Pam had entered the contest.

Pam had learned that the model chosen for the Midwest region was a student at Wilder University. Company reps would be on campus next week to announce the name of the girl—possibly her own!

"I know what you're thinking," Jamal accused her, pointing a playful finger at her when the music stopped. He grabbed her around the waist and lifted her off the ground. "I know."

"Do not," Pam squealed, wriggling away.

"You're just thinking about all those cameras and all that attention," he teased. Pam was glad Jamal seemed to have gotten over his jealousy of Jesse Potter, the cute rep for Natural Shades who Jamal had thought was hitting on Pam.

Pam just laughed and hugged him around the waist. Of course she was excited. The Natural Shades announcement would be fun. And Jesse would be coming, too. Sure, her friend Reva Ross was also up for the contract, but she was glad they both had a shot at it now. Whoever won would earn plenty of money for school and have a great time doing it.

"Gail's on the warpath with this story," Jake was saying, stirring a batch of spaghetti sauce on the top of his stove. "She wants *everyone* working on it next week from all different angles."

"I was hoping for a week of serenity," Nancy drawled. She leaned back in a kitchen chair. "Fat chance. Whew, it's been crazy lately."

Jake grinned at her and tasted the sauce. "Yeah, but you sure had that Greg Pawling pegged. Gail wrote up the story today. What a creep."

Nancy shook her head. "He didn't seem like the type. Actually, he seemed like a pretty nice guy at first."

"Mmmm," Jake said.

Nancy whistled. "Well, I'm glad he was caught and all the loan money was retrieved." She put her feet up on the chair next to her. "So, brief me on this investigative story Gail's working on."

"Okay," Jake replied, filling a big pot of water, and setting it on the stove. Jake spent a few minutes telling Nancy about Gail's story and the case it involved.

"Whoa," Nancy said when he'd finished. "This sounds like a great news story. A controversial sexual molestation and robbery case being reopened right here in little old Weston."

Jake nodded, popping an olive into his mouth.

"Gail's been doing a ton of digging on the case and says it's going to be a bombshell of a story."

"That's why she's a wreck." Nancy shook her head. "I saw her today in the newsroom, and she looked like she hadn't eaten anything in days. I brought her a cup of coffee and a sandwich."

Jake chuckled. "Don't feel sorry, Nancy. This is as good as it gets for Gail. She's dancing in the streets over this." Jake jumped down as his water started boiling. He opened a package of spaghetti and dumped it in.

"Mind if I phone Dad from here?" Nancy asked. "I've put off calling him for too long."

"Dinner in about fifteen minutes."

Nancy found Jake's portable phone and quickly punched in her father's number. Then she turned around and faced the window, watching the dark outline of trees against the evening sky. "Dad?"

"Nancy!" her dad answered. "Hello!"

"Crazy week, Dad," Nancy explained. "I'm sorry I couldn't talk. I had to help George with some loan problems. And I had a ton of studying and articles for the *Times*."

"Don't apologize, Nancy," Carson replied. There was a short silence on the other end of the line, and she could hear her dad clearing his throat. "I just—well, I guess I just wanted to talk with you a little about Avery—"

"Oh, Dad—" Nancy interrupted.

"No, no, no," Carson broke in. "There was a lot of tension in the house last weekend, and I thought it would be good to talk things over. Just as we always do."

Nancy clasped her forehead. Her dad was so cool about things. "You're right, Dad."

"So," Carson said firmly. "Tell me how you feel about Avery. Is there a problem? Is there something we can do to—*I* can do, to make you feel more comfortable with our—friendship?"

Nancy bit her lip, feeling more terrible by the minute. Her dad had finally found a woman to love, and he was calling her up to practically ask for her permission. "No, Dad. Everything's fine with Avery," she lied. "I—I was just a little off balance that weekend, with Paul Cody's death so fresh in my mind and Bess so upset. I'm sorry about everything."

Nancy swiveled in her chair and saw Jake staring sharply at her.

"Okay, Nancy," her dad went along. "Just checking. Now, tell me about George. Something about a loan problem?"

Nancy explained the details. By the time she rang off, Jake was piling spaghetti onto two plates. Nancy stood up and began slicing a loaf of French bread, but she saw the tension in Jake's face. "Oh, stop looking at me that way," Nancy suddenly snapped.

Jake shrugged. "Okay. I shouldn't have listened to your phone conversation. I don't like to hear someone lie to her father."

"I wasn't lying!" Nancy exploded.

Jake spun around and faced her, gripping a

container of Parmesan cheese in one hand. "Oh, pardon me. That was the *truth* you were telling your father a few minutes ago. 'Everything's fine with Avery. Oh yes. Fine. Great.' "

"Stop it, Jake!" Nancy cried. "You don't understand."

"Nope."

"Then forget it."

"I can't forget it, Nancy," Jake said, trying to keep his voice under control. "When I ask you for the truth, is that what you give me, too? Lies? How can I ever trust you if you're so worried about hurting people's feelings that you can't bring yourself to speak the truth? I'm sorry, Nancy, but I hate that."

"Listen, Jake." Nancy tried to calm down. "I love my father, and I don't want to throw cold water on his relationship with Avery just because I'm having trouble with it."

Jake put his hands on his hips and stared off into space.

"Okay?" Nancy nudged him. "Let's not argue about this, Jake. Maybe I'm wrong. Maybe you're wrong. But let's drop it for now and talk about something else."

Jake grudgingly slipped his hands around her waist and pulled her playfully close. "Don't want to spoil our evening, huh? That's good, because I've been slaving over a hot stove."

Nancy looked up at him and held out her right hand. "Truce?"

"Truce," Jake answered, leaning down and

dropping a kiss on her mouth. "I'm glad our fights don't last long."

Nancy just sighed.

"Want to go dancing tonight?" Jake suggested, swaying her back and forth, then suddenly dipping her back from the waist. He held her tightly with his strong arms.

"Where?" Nancy cried out, laughing. Her head was flung back, and she was seeing everything upside down.

"The Underground," Jake whispered, pulling her back up again. "After we eat our spaghetti and you let me kiss you."

"In that order?" Nancy teased.

"No," Jake grabbed her again, this time giving her an even longer kiss. "In this order, Nancy."

Next in Nancy Drew on Campus™:

All her life Stephanie's been looking for a guy like Jonathan. But now that she's found him, she's going out of her way to mess up—and finding plenty of guys willing to help. Bess, meanwhile, can't get past the tragic loss of her boyfriend. But she may find the comfort and support she needs in the most surprising place. *The* place to be, though, is Club Z and Nancy wants to check it out. She's working on an exposé for *Wilder Times* that could put her at odds with her editor *and* with Jake. Everybody's feeling the pressure, and opening night at the club will be the time to blow off steam or blow the lid off all the secrets on campus . . . in *Keeping Secrets,* Nancy Drew on Campus #18.